Christmas in My Heart® 27

Joe L. Wheeler

Pacific Press® Publishing Association

Nampa, Idaho | Oshawa, Ontario, Canada
www.pacificpress.com

Copyright © 2018 by Joe L. Wheeler
Printed in the United States of America
All rights reserved

Cover design by Steve Lanto
Cover art by Dorothy Angell
Interior illustrations from the library of Joe L. Wheeler
Series design: cover and interior by Helcio Deslandes

The author assumes full responsibility for the accuracy of all facts and quotations as cited in this book.

Christmas in My Heart® is a registered trademark of Joe L. Wheeler and may not be used by anyone else in any form. Visit Joe Wheeler's website at www.joewheelerbooks.com. Representing the author is WordServe Literary Group, Ltd., 7500 E. Arapahoe Road, Suite 285, Centennial, CO 80112.

Additional copies of this book are available by calling toll-free 1-800-765-6955 or by visiting www.AdventistBookCenter.com.

None of these stories may be reprinted or placed on the Internet without the express written permission of the editor/compiler, Joe L. Wheeler (PO Box 1246, Conifer, CO 80433), or the copyright holder.

Library of Congress Cataloging-in-Publication Data:

Wheeler, Joe L., 1936–   comp.
   Christmas in my heart. Book 27.
   1. Christmas stories, American. I. Title:
Christmas in my heart. Book 27.

ISBN: 978-0-8163-6268-4

May 2018

Dedication

FOR OUR ONE HUNDREDTH BOOK

As I look back through the years, searching for the one person who has done more than anyone else to make our books (more than 1,500,000 copies) possible, it turned out to be no contest.

- She has orchestrated 27 years worth of correspondence.
- She has coordinated 27 years of book orders.
- By the end of this year, she will have typed and posted 481 weekly blogs and 2,650 daily quotation tweets.
- She has typed 98 of our one hundred books. Specifically (in published books), including

Doubleday/Random House (1,343 pages)
Mission Books (840 pages)
Focus on the Family/Tyndale House (10,784 pages)
Guideposts (746 pages)
Howard/Simon & Schuster (1,495 pages)
Thomas Nelson (1,210 pages)
Pacific Press and Review and Herald (6,008 pages)
WaterBrook/Random House (951 pages)
Books in translation (Spanish, Indonesian, Polish, Norwegian; totaling 2,317 pages)

Altogether, an astounding 26,623 pages! In many cases, multiple times. For instance, she typed the 612-page *Quo Vadis* five times. Besides all this, she has remained by my side, in good times and bad, for 58 years, in the process raising two children we are so proud of. Because of all this—and ever so much more—it gives me great joy to dedicate *Christmas in My Heart 27* to my beloved bride, cherished friend, incurable fellow traveler, quilter-in-residence (70 and counting—all hand-quilted), and publishing partner:

CONNIE PALMER WHEELER

Books by Joe L. Wheeler

Abraham Lincoln: A Man of Faith and Courage
Abraham Lincoln Civil War Stories: Heartwarming Stories About Our Most Beloved President
Amelia, the Flying Squirrel and Other Great Stories of God's Smallest Creatures
Best of Christmas in My Heart, 1, 2
Bluegrass Girl, A
Candle in the Forest and Other Christmas Stories Children Love
Christmas in My Heart®, books 1–27
Christmas in My Heart Treasuries (4)
Christmas in My Heart, audio books 1–6
Christmas in My Soul, gift books (3)
Dick, the Babysitting Bear and Other Great Wild Animal Stories
Easter in My Heart
Everyday Heroes
Great Stories Remembered, I, II, III
Great Stories Remembered, audio books I–III
Great Stories Remembered Classic Books (12 books)
Heart to Heart Stories for Dads
Heart to Heart Stories for Moms
Heart to Heart Stories of Friendship
Heart to Heart Stories for Grandparents
Heart to Heart Stories of Love
Heart to Heart Stories for Sisters
Heart to Heart Stories for Teachers
Mother's Face Is Her Child's First Heaven, A
My Favorite Angel Stories
My Favorite Courage Stories
My Favorite Life-Changing Stories
My Favorite Miracle Stories
My Favorite Prayer Stories
Only God Can Make a Dad
Owney, the Post Office Dog and Other Great Dog Stories
Remote Controlled
Saint Nicholas (a Thomas Nelson Christian Encounter biography)
Showdown and Other Sports Stories for Boys
Smoky, the Ugliest Cat in the World and Other Great Cat Stories
Spot, the Dog That Broke the Rules and Other Great Heroic Animal Stories
St. Nicholas: A Closer Look at Christmas (with Canon James Rosenthal)
Stinky, the Skunk That Wouldn't Leave and Other Strange and Wonderful Animal Stories
Soldier Stories
Sooty, the Green-Eyed Kitten and Other Great Animal Stories
Stories of Angels Seen and Unseen
Tawny, the Magnificent Jaguar and Other Great Jungle Stories
Tears of Joy for Mothers
Time for a Story
Togo, the Sled Dog and Other Great Animal Stories of the North
Twelve Stories of Christmas, The
What's So Good About Tough Times?
Wildfire, the Red Stallion and Other Great Horse Stories
Wings of God, The
Zane Grey's Impact on American Life and Letters
Zane Grey's Master Character Index

Acknowledgments

Frontispiece poem, "Travelers From the East," by Emma A. Lente. Published in *St. Nicholas Magazine*, December 1907. Original text owned by Joe Wheeler.

Introduction: "The Mysterious Star of Bethlehem," by Franklyn M. Branley and Joseph Leininger Wheeler. Branley's study was originally given as a lecture at the famed Hayden Planetarium in New York. It was later published in *Redbook*, in December 1966. That same year, it was also published in book form by Thomas Y. Crowell Company. Original texts of both the magazine and the book owned by Joe Wheeler. If anyone can provide information on the author's next of kin, please relay information to Joe Wheeler (PO Box 1246, Conifer, CO 80433).

"Five Days Before Christmas," by Hope Hale. Published in *Redbook*, December 1959. Original text owned by Joe Wheeler. If anyone can provide information on the author or the next of kin, please relay information to Joe Wheeler (PO Box 1246, Conifer, CO 80433).

"Christmas on the *Mayflower*," by Elizabeth Cady Stanton. Published in *St. Nicholas*, December 1900. Original text owned by Joe Wheeler.

"Home, Sweet Home," by Malone Hobson. Published in *The People's Home Journal*, December 1921. Original text owned by Joe Wheeler.

"We Two, Together," by Mary Russell. Published in *Young People's Weekly*, December 20, 1936. Reprinted by permission of Joe Wheeler (PO Box 1246, Conifer, CO 80433) and David C. Cook (4050 Vance View, Colorado Springs, CO 80918).

"The Red Glass Bowl," by Margaret Weymouth Jackson. Published in *Good Housekeeping*, December 1931. Original text owned by Joe Wheeler.

"The Christmas Year," by Rebecca Harding Davis. Published in *St. Nicholas*, December 1907. Original text owned by Joe Wheeler.

"The Little Brown House," by Marie Conway Oemler. Published in *Woman's Home Companion*, December 1912. Original text owned by Joe Wheeler.

"Home for Christmas," by Maude W. Plummer. Published in *This Day*, December 1956. Original text owned by Joe Wheeler. If anyone can provide information on the author or the next of kin, please relay information to Joe Wheeler (PO Box 1246, Conifer, CO 80433).

"Christmas Tonight," by Val Teal. Published in *Child Life*, December 1946. Original text owned by Joe Wheeler. If anyone can provide information on the author or the next of kin, please relay information to Joe Wheeler (PO Box 1246, Conifer, CO 80433).

"The Five O'clock Train," by Ina Brevoort Roberts. Published in *Woman's Home Companion*, December 1911. Original text owned by Joe Wheeler.

"Christmas Bell," by Adeline Rumsey. Published in *Woman's Home Companion*, December 1943. Original text owned by Joe Wheeler. If anyone can provide information on the author or the next of kin, please relay information to Joe Wheeler (PO Box 1246, Conifer, CO 80433).

"Christmas Eve," by Kathleen Coyle. Published in *Redbook*, December 1951. Original text owned by Joe Wheeler. If anyone can provide information on the author or the next of kin, please relay information to Joe Wheeler (PO Box 1246, Conifer, CO 80433).

"Appointment in the Desert," by Margaret Cousins. Published in *Redbook*, December, 1954. Original text owned by Joe Wheeler. If anyone can provide information on the author or the next of kin, please relay information to Joe Wheeler (P.O. Box 1246, Conifer, CO 80433).

" 'Merry Christmas, Miss Blakely,' " by Linda Stevens Almond. Published in *St. Nicholas*, December 1919. Original text owned by Joe Wheeler.

"God Works in Mysterious Ways," by Joseph Leininger Wheeler. Copyright © 2017. Printed by permission of the author.

Contents

Frontispiece poem—"Travelers From the East" 8
Emma A. Lente

Introduction: The Mysterious Star of Bethlehem 9
Joseph Leininger Wheeler and Franklyn M. Branley

Five Days Before Christmas 15
Hope Hale

Christmas on the *Mayflower* 24
Elizabeth Cady Stanton

Home, Sweet Home 27
Malone Hobson

We Two, Together 33
Mary Russell

The Red Glass Bowl 38
Margaret Weymouth Jackson

The Christmas Year 49
Rebecca Harding Davis

The Little Brown House 51
Marie Conway Oemler

Home for Christmas 62
Maude W. Plummer

Christmas Tonight 68
Val Teal

The Five-O'clock Train 73
Ina Brevoort Roberts

Christmas Bell 79
Adeline Rumsey

Christmas Eve 89
Kathleen Coyle

Appointment in the Desert 92
Margaret Cousins

"Merry Christmas, Miss Blakely!" 101
Linda Stevens Almond

God Works in Mysterious Ways 109
Joseph Leininger Wheeler

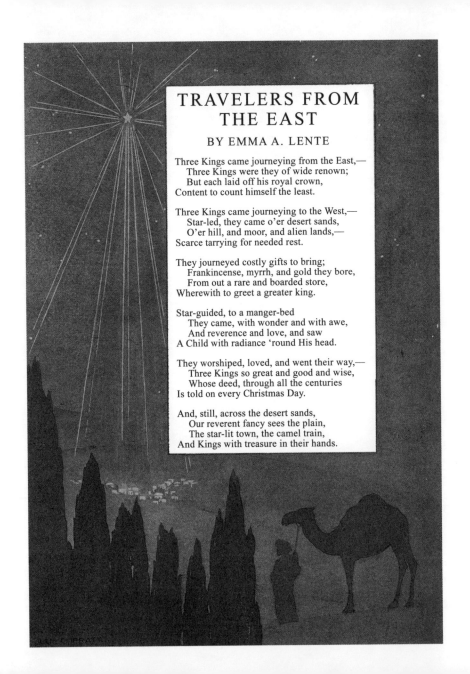

TRAVELERS FROM THE EAST

BY EMMA A. LENTE

Three Kings came journeying from the East,—
    Three Kings were they of wide renown;
    But each laid off his royal crown,
Content to count himself the least.

Three Kings came journeying to the West,—
    Star-led, they came o'er desert sands,
    O'er hill, and moor, and alien lands,—
Scarce tarrying for needed rest.

They journeyed costly gifts to bring;
    Frankincense, myrrh, and gold they bore,
    From out a rare and boarded store,
Wherewith to greet a greater king.

Star-guided, to a manger-bed
    They came, with wonder and with awe,
    And reverence and love, and saw
A Child with radiance 'round His head.

They worshiped, loved, and went their way,—
    Three Kings so great and good and wise,
    Whose deed, through all the centuries
Is told on every Christmas Day.

And, still, across the desert sands,
    Our reverent fancy sees the plain,
    The star-lit town, the camel train,
And Kings with treasure in their hands.

INTRODUCTION

The Mysterious Star of Bethlehem

Joseph Leininger Wheeler and Franklyn M. Branley

As I think back through the past twenty-six years and the thousands of Christmas stories I have read, and the 417 we have anthologized in this series, I am struck by the ubiquitousness of the Star of Bethlehem. After all, the Star is essential to any retelling of the Nativity story.

Although many writers have speculated about the Star's origin, no one appears to have ever exhaustively studied it in a scholarly way—until Dr. Franklyn M. Branley's landmark study, first presented as a lecture at the famed Hayden Planetarium in New York. In 1966, the lecture was printed in the December issue of *Redbook* and as a self-standing book published by Thomas Y. Crowell Company. Branley would go on to write more than 200 books. At the time of that lecture, Branley was educational director; he would go on to become director of the entire Hayden Planetarium Center.

When I shared all this with my wife, Connie, she felt it was so significant, and of such potential value to all those who treasure Christmas stories, that it ought to be given the lead position in our twenty-seventh collection. So here it is, after half a century of being all but forgotten—we are sharing it with you verbatim.

THE CHRISTMAS SKY

Now when Jesus was born in Bethlehem of Judaea in the days of Herod the King, behold, there came wise men from the east to Jerusalem, saying, Where is he that is born King of the Jews? for we have seen his star in the east, and are come to worship him.
—Matthew 2:1, 2

* * * * *

The coming of Jesus marked the beginning of Christianity. Since His birth His teachings have spread around the world, and millions have found happiness by learning His lessons and living in the way He directed.

We know only one story of the birth of Jesus, the one told in the Bible; if others were written, they do not exist today. For 1,000 years and more, historians, scholars, priests and astronomers have tried to find out more about His birth—the first Christmas—an event so important, it changed the history of the world.

The star that the Wise Men followed to Bethlehem—the "star in the east"—has been a clue for astronomers, and they have tried to pinpoint its appearance. In doing so they have put together evidence that Christ's birth took place several years before the year we now call anno Domini I—the first year of our Lord.

Astronomers know that the Star of Bethlehem is no longer in the sky; yet 2,000 years ago men gazed at the same stars we see today. The theory has been advanced that the "star" may not have been a star at all. Several possibilities have been suggested to explain the light in the sky that guided the Magi. Could it have been a meteor, or a comet, or a new star coming

INTRODUCTION

to birth at about the same time as Jesus?

It seems unlikely that the star of Bethlehem was a meteor. These streaks of light that are also called shooting stars are made when small bits of material, sometimes as light and feathery as ashes, enter our atmosphere and become heated. But they last only for seconds; and the Christmas star would have had to remain in the sky for weeks and perhaps months, all through the time it took the Wise Men to make their long journey to Bethlehem.

It is unlikely, too, that the star was a comet. Comets are wispy, cloudlike formations of gases and cosmic dust that reflect sunlight. They are members of the solar system and, like planets, are held in regular orbits by the attraction of the sun. Frequently they are large and bright enough to be seen clearly without a telescope, and they may remain visible for several days, weeks, sometimes months. But since the paths of comets can be figured as accurately as those of planets, astronomers know which ones were close enough to the earth to be seen thousands of years ago; there was no bright comet visible around the time of Jesus' birth. In any case, comets were believed to be the finger of a god pointing toward the earth, warning of danger and calamity. They were associated with famines and floods, earthquakes and disasters—never with happy events.

* * * * *

In 1604 the German astronomer Johannes Kepler suggested a third possibility. He saw a star one night where there had been no star before. It grew brighter and brighter until finally it could be seen in the daylight. Then it faded and rapidly disappeared. Such a star is called a *nova*, from the Latin word for "new," and Kepler thought that the Star of Bethlehem might have been a nova. But modern astronomers can trace the appearance of new stars down through history, and there was no nova in the sky anywhere near the time we believe Jesus was born.

Around A.D. 93, a man called Flavius Josephus wrote a history of the Jewish people. In it he described certain events that occurred near the time of Jesus' birth.

"Now, it happened that during the high priesthood of Matthias, there was another person made high priest for a single day, that very day which the Jews observe as a feast, and that very night there was an eclipse of the moon."

The new high priest, according to Josephus, was appointed because of the sickness of King Herod, a brief sickness of which the king shortly died. The Bible tells us that Herod was king of Jerusalem at the time of Jesus' birth. The feast to which Josephus refers was probably Purim, a Jewish religious observance. Because Josephus reports that the feast was held at a time when an eclipse occurred, we have a clue to the time of Herod's death. On March 13th, in the year now referred to as 4 B.C.—before the birth of Christ—there was a partial eclipse of the moon, the only one that occurred on or near any religious festival day for several years on either side of 4 B.C. Herod therefore must have died a short time after March 13 in 4 B.C. According to these calculations, Jesus must have been born in 4 B.C.—or earlier.

In the Bible we pick up further clues as to just how much earlier it might have been. Herod had heard of the birth of Jesus and feared the prophecy of His power. He commanded the Wise Men who were seeking the birthplace of Jesus to be

INTRODUCTION

brought before him in Jerusalem, and asked them to return to him after they had found the child. Then Herod himself could go to honor Him.

But the Wise Men did not return to Jerusalem. The Bible says that angels came to warn them that Herod planned to destroy Jesus; they returned to their country by another route.

Herod, angered by their disobedience and fearful of the infant child, ordered a brutal murder. According to Matthew, chapter 2, verse 16:

> Then Herod, when he saw that he was mocked of the wise men, was exceeding wroth, and sent forth, and slew all the children that were in Bethlehem, and in all the coasts thereof, from two years old and under, according to the time which he had diligently inquired of the wise men.

We do not know exactly how long it was from the time when Herod saw the Wise Men until the time when they were to return to Jerusalem to report to him. But it must have been no longer than two years in order for Herod to assume that Jesus would be among the children whose death he ordered.

There is still another clue in the Bible that Jesus was born sometime before A.D. 1. In chapter 2, verses 1–7, of the Gospel according to St. Luke we read:

> And it came to pass in those days, that there went out a decree from Caesar Augustus, that all the world should be taxed. . . . And all went to be taxed, every one into his own city. And Joseph also went up from Galilee, out of the city of Nazareth, into Judaea, unto the city of David, which is called Bethlehem; (because he was of the house and lineage of David:) to be taxed with Mary his espoused wife, being great with child. And so it was, that, while they were there, the days were accomplished that she should be delivered. And she brought forth her firstborn son, and wrapped him in swaddling clothes, and laid him in a manger; because there was no room for them in the inn.

Two thousand years ago the Roman Empire spread all around the Mediterranean Sea, and every person within it was subject to its taxes. During the reign of Caesar Augustus, three tax orders were sent out to the people. This is known from the inscription on a stone tablet uncovered in 1923 by archaeologists working near Ankara, Turkey. The tablet, an inscription from a Roman temple, was a record of many events of the time, including the three great tax orders. One of the orders was issued in the year we call 8 B.C. For the tax to be levied, each person had to return to his birthplace so he could be counted and the tax collected. Joseph and Mary, along with all the others, crowded into Judaea and the small city of Bethlehem, known as the city of David.

* * * * *

The tax order issued in 8 B.C. strengthens the theory that Jesus was born at least two years later. News was slow to travel in those days, and tax collections were not made everywhere at the same time. Collectors journeyed from village to village, counting the people, charging the taxes, and collecting the

INTRODUCTION

money. They took months and even years to reach the outer boundaries of the empire. People returning to the place where they were born traveled overland by foot or by donkey. Their journeys, too, were tedious and long. Many months might pass between the time people first heard of the order and their arrival in the city of their birth.

The events around the time of Herod's death and the records of the tax orders of Caesar Augustus lead to the same conclusion: Jesus was born sometime between 8 B.C. and 4 B.C.—probably in the year 6 B.C.

The celebration of Christmas on December 25th has less to do with the date of the birth than with other circumstances of the times. In the early days of Christianity it was a crime to be a Christian, and those who followed Christ's teachings did so in secret. Since they could not reveal their identities, secret places to worship and secret ways to celebrate the Nativity had to be devised. Small groups would meet together in the cold and dark of the catacombs, which were burial places beneath the streets of Rome. Some groups celebrated Christmas on a Roman festival day that came during the Saturnalia, a period of gaiety during which gifts were exchanged, people danced in the streets and decorated their homes with flowers and boughs. The climax of the Saturnalia occurred on December 25. Because all Rome was joyful on this day, Christians used it to mark Christ's birth so that their own joyous celebration would be overlooked in the excitement of the general festivities.

December 25 had been an important day since ancient times, when men worshiped the sun. As fall and winter approached, the noonday sun sank lower on the horizon and plants began to die in the fields. Men grew afraid that the sun would disappear completely, and for several days toward the middle of December, when the sun was lowest, celebrations were held to keep the sun god from leaving the sky. Consequently the first day of winter was the time of greatest joy, for after that the sun rose higher and higher with the passing of each day.

According to our present calendar, the first day of winter is on December 21st or 22nd, but there have been many different calendars through the centuries. On one ancient calendar winter began on December 25th, and it was by this calendar that the Saturnalia was celebrated.

In the early part of the fourth century the persecution of the Christians ended. It was the emperor Constantine, a convert to Christianity, who decreed that the birth of Jesus should be celebrated on December 25th. But Jesus' birth probably occurred in the spring. In chapter 2, verse 8, of the Gospel according to St. Luke we learn:

> And there were in the same country shepherds abiding
> in the field, keeping watch over their flock by night.

In Judaea the month of December is cold and rainy. At that time flocks are taken into corrals to be sheltered, and only in the spring do the shepherds keep watch through the night in the fields, for it is then that the newborn lambs need their protection.

The accumulated evidence from the Bible and from the writings of Josephus makes it reasonable to assume that Jesus was born in the spring of the year 6 B.C. The tables of motions and positions of planets show that there were three planets in the evening skies in the fall and winter of 7 B.C. continuing into the spring of 6 B.C., and that these planets moved closer

INTRODUCTION

together as the months went by.

The planets were Mars, Jupiter and Saturn. Saturn was in the constellation of Pisces, the fishes. Jupiter was a bit below and to the north. Mars was much lower and toward the south.

As the winter of 7 B.C. and the early months of 6 B.C. passed, the three planets moved closer and closer together, and in the late winter and early spring they formed a small triangle in the constellation Pisces. However, the triangle could not be easily seen because the planets were low in the western sky, and they set beneath the horizon before full darkness came.

But the Magi were astrologers and knew about the positions and motions of planets. They knew that the three planets were in a constellation where centuries earlier, according to Jewish rabbis, planets had appeared three years previous to the birth of Moses, the prophet who was to return the Israelites out of Egypt to the eastern borders of the Promised Land. Pisces was therefore considered the national constellation of the Jews as well as a tribal symbol. It may have been a sign to the Magi that an event of great importance was occurring in the land of the Jews, and the three planets, close together in Pisces, may have been the Star of Bethlehem that the Wise Men followed to the manger.

* * * * *

But there are many persons who believe that the Star of Bethlehem was neither a group of planets nor an exploding star nor an especially brilliant meteor or comet. To them the star was like nothing men had ever seen before. They believed it was a miracle.

A confluence of three planets—or a miracle? Probably we will never know what the Star of Christmas really was. But no matter what it might have been, the sign that appeared in the sky that first Christmas will always have deep meaning for millions of people. For the coming of Jesus brought a promise of peace on earth and good will to men.

* * * * *

About this collection

One of my major concerns, in recent years, has to do with the imperative necessity of tracking down new stories each year so that readers would see each new collection as new and vital, not merely a gentle coasting downhill from the previous year's high. Without these yearly transfusions of stories new to us, readership would inevitably decrease each year.

Now keep in mind the sad reality that precious few great Christmas stories are being written these days. Consequently, we are forced to sift through the musty old pages of family magazines that flourished during what I call the Golden Age of Judeo-Christian Stories (roughly 1880's through the 1950's). The advent of television and the mass media (post World War II) accelerated the demise of these magazines. But successive nails in their coffins were the assassinations of John F. Kennedy, Robert Kennedy, Martin Luther King, and Malcolm X, followed by the resulting uproar in our streets, and the devastating disillusion spawned by the Vietnam War.

As a result, once again Connie and I turned to Golden Age magazines, accessing for the very first time the eBay arena. Not by any means a cheap way to purchase vintage magazines! But the expenses proved more than worth it: two-thirds of this

INTRODUCTION

new collection came from eBay purchases (a number involving auction bidding). We thereby unearthed powerful Christmas stories we'd never read before. We hope and pray they may be a blessing to you, your families, your churches, and your schools.

The startling result? For the first time ever, only one author (Margaret Weymouth Jackson) of the fourteen stories (other than my own) had been featured before: every other author is new to this series!

Coda

I always look forward to hearing from you! Please do keep the stories, responses, and suggestions coming—and not just for Christmas stories. I am putting together collections of other genres as well. You may reach me by writing to:

> Joe L. Wheeler, PhD
> PO Box 1246
> Conifer, CO 80433

May the Lord bless and guide the ministry of these stories in your home.

Franklyn M. Branley (1915–2002), author of over 200 books, joined the staff of the famed American Museum - Hayden Planetarium in September 1956 as head of the planetarium education program. In 1968, Dr. Branley was elected chairman of the Hayden, and remained in that position until his retirement. Perhaps his greatest direct impact on astronomy was a program sponsored by the National Science Foundation. It was a two-week summer adventure for top-level high school students with a strong interest in science, especially astronomy—it proved to be so successful that the National Science Foundation sponsored it for thirteen years rather than their usual three.

Five Days Before Christmas

Hope Hale

Martha was busy—Martha like-in-the-Bible busy—for Christmas was just around the corner. And there were so many things she had to do before then.

Then little Philip crumpled on the front porch—unable to move, and had to be carried up to bed. His forehead was hot. No, she thought, not just before Christmas!

* * * * *

Perhaps the last package would never be wrapped, or bought, but the pure joy of giving came to her five days before Christmas.

* * * * *

The first snow had fallen in the night, covering the lawn with a lavish layer of soft rich white, like the cream frosting on the spice cake Martha had made for the bazaar. The children were utterly out of hand. A white Christmas! But would it last six days? Would it even last till after school? Did they—"Oh, please not, Mommie!"—really have to go to school?

Martha kept answering their questions firmly, trying not to sound impatient—she *had* to get them out of the house—answering all the questions but her husband's. Walter's she could not really hear. It was the waiting look in his eyes as he stood there by the door, big and solid in his gray overcoat, his briefcase under his arm, keys swinging from one finger as he watched her struggle with Philip's boot. The little boy sat listlessly on the lowest step, his head pressed against the wall.

"Mom!" Sandy stamped in from testing the snow. "Put a coat of lacquer on my skis, will you, so it'll dry before—"

She might have laughed, or cried, it was so fantastic. "I have to make cinnamon rolls." She controlled her voice. "And you have to mail those last packages, Sandy, after school. Remember, they're late because you forgot to fire your ashtrays—"

His father said tentatively, "Seems a shame to waste the snow. . . ."

Martha drew a deep breath. She expected to carry the Christmas load, but for him to *add* to her burden . . .

"The last bell's just about to *ring*!" Prilly cried.

"I'll take the kids," Walter said, "if you're sure you—"

The phone rang.

"Oh, take them!" Martha went to answer the phone.

The older children hurried out. Walter pulled Philip to his feet and left. On the telephone Mrs. Carhart talked on about desertions from the committee. She had tried to get Mrs. Todd, whose children were grown up, but she could not come because Mr. T. had to speak in Marbury and she was driving over the Notch with him. "Not to shop, mind you!" Mrs. Carhart said bitterly. "Just to see the snow on the pine trees! She must be mighty scared of losing the Reverend, the way she tags after him!"

Martha had a sudden vision of Pauline Todd, her brown eyes shining below the silvery hair, her lips laughing like a girl's, turning to her husband as they rode through the snow. She felt an absurd pang.

"I'll relieve you for two hours," she told Mrs. Carhart, "while Philip's at his rehearsal."

* * * * *

Then at last she was in the kitchen, clearing away breakfast, laying out butter and sugar and flour, but not efficiently. It was as if Walter still stood there, swinging his keys, waiting.

She recalled his few words and her hand stopped still. He had wanted to know if she needed the car. He would have walked to his law office through a mile of heavy snow if she had said the word. And she had not answered.

But she had, really. She had told Sandy about the baking. But Walter became deaf when she talked of tasks—deaf or worse. Like last night, when he had found her ironing a red ribbon and she had explained: "Prilly's ashamed of our front door without a wreath."

"Let *her* hang one, then." He had made it sound so easy. She had told him how she planned to use a spray of artificial flowers from an old evening dress and had gilded a toy trumpet of Philip's. He had merely compressed his lips and, after a moment, gone upstairs.

When at last she had crept into bed, he stirred, half asleep, and reached out for her. But she lay stiffly on her side, her limbs tense and aching. Her mind had spun with lists and schedules all night long.

* * * * *

The children came home for lunch as she took the cinnamon rolls from the oven. "Fe-fi-fo-fum!" Sandy shouted. "I smell something yum!"

Prilly came to sniff, her blue eyes shining, her fair hair curling from under her dark blue hood.

"I'm afraid they're not for us," Martha said reluctantly.

The light in Prilly's eyes dimmed. Sandy groaned.

"Where's Philip?" Martha asked.

"On the front step," Prilly said. "We couldn't get him in."

Martha swooped out to get Philip, the icy wind catching her throat, and brought him into the kitchen. He slumped in a chair, his hand supporting his head. His face was flushed and his eyelids were half closed.

"Don't you feel well, Phil?" She touched his forehead and felt the shock of heat.

"Shall I take him up to bed?" Sandy asked, beside her.

She nodded. Her knees felt too weak to carry her own weight upstairs.

Running for the thermometer, Martha heard a sound and knew she had heard it before: a harsh, barking cough. But this morning she had not noticed; she had been too busy.

Philip did not resist the glass rod under his tongue. He lay on his bed as if pressed into the mattress. She warned herself against panic, walking to the phone. Even if he did have a temperature, it might be nothing.

Dr. Joe was out on calls. His nurse would have him phone. Martha stifled an impulse to phone Walter; he would soon be home.

Philip coughed. She could make a steam tent of his bunk,

she decided, and asked Prilly to put water on the stove. "And, oh, your soup—"

"I've already hotted it. Shall I bring up you and Phil some?"

"Not yet." Martha heard her voice soften. "And you and Sandy have some cinnamon rolls."

They start to whoop and checked themselves. Martha went to the linen closet, got sheets, pinned them as curtains to the upper bunk. The phone rang. "Oh, Mrs. Carhart," she heard Prilly say, "Mother can't. My little brother's ill." Prilly could have been thirty, from her voice, instead of eleven. But she giggled as she came up the stairs. "Mrs. Carhart said, 'Hum.'" She peered in at Philip. "Mother! He's going to be sick!"

Philip's flush had faded to greenish pallor. His hands clutched at the covers. Prilly brought the basin just in time.

* * * * *

As Philip lay back on the pillows, exhausted, Martha wiped his forehead and told Prilly, "It must be the twenty-four-hour thing. If he's better tomorrow, I may still be able to carry on with—with—" Well, with whatever she had been so busy doing.

"He's just *got* to be well by Christmas," Prilly breathed.

Oh, yes, that was it: shopping, gifts . . .

"After all, our Christmas is only *for* him, really," Prilly added.

Martha turned to look astonished, into the anxious little face. Could this be Prilly, who had presented her list like an ultimatum, decorated freely with asterisks which

17

referred to a footnote reading, "absolutely essential"?

Remotely, from another world, the school bell rang. The sound of a shovel scraping on concrete stopped abruptly. The door opened downstairs. "Prilly, come on!" Sandy shouted. "It's time."

Prilly started, then stopped. "I'll tell Miss Mikkelson," she said to her mother. "I can take your place decorating. Elspeth and Cathy will help."

"But don't you have a rehearsal too?" Martha asked, a little dazed.

"The heavenly chorus always has to wait for hours," Prilly explained kindly, as to a child. Then she was gone, leaving Martha suddenly, helplessly alone.

* * * * *

In the silence there was only one sound: Philip's breathing. Wasn't it too fast? Yes, far too fast; there was an urgency about it, as if he drew each breath in haste, for fear— She jumped up quickly and began to tidy the room, snatching up scattered socks, model planes, comic books, her movements jerkily mechanical.

The door opened downstairs and she heard Walter's step on the stairs. The house felt warmer, no longer empty.

"The kids told me," he said in the doorway. He came in and laid his hand on Philip's forehead. "Feels pretty hot and dry."

"I'd better take his temperature again," she said.

Walter did not protest as she had expected. He asked, "Isn't he breathing—well—fast?"

She held her hand firm on the thermometer. "I—I don't know." They waited silent minutes.

"At his age," Walter said low over her shoulder, "temperatures don't necessarily mean a thing."

Was he trying to reassure her or was he asking reassurance? She tried to give it to him with a smile, looking up at him.

His hand moved a little, touched her cheek. She caught it, held it, leaned against him. The contact with his solidness through the rough cloth of his suit steadied her. She drew out the thermometer and saw the bright long line: 103.4.

The phone rang; it would be the doctor. Walter answered, and she felt hysteria rise in her as he said, "Rolls, cake? Uh, sure. Be there in an hour."

Then he called the doctor's number and gave the facts with masculine economy. But he added quietly, "Joe, look— we'll feel a lot better when you see the boy."

She heard him moving around the kitchen. Then he appeared with a tray. "Eat this soup, kid," he told her gruffly. He hadn't called her that since Sandy was born.

"What about you?" she asked.

"I'll have Karl send over something from the diner," he said. "I have to take one last glance at Gronowalski versus Fullerton Trucking Corporation."

"You're not going into court?" she cried.

He nodded. The case had been postponed half a dozen times since the morning two years ago when Stan Gronowalski, eighteen years old, six feet tall and blond, had been crushed against the wall of his father's barn by the truck he was loading with potatoes. He had been left badly crippled. The trucking company had offered five hundred dollars as compensation, and this insult had brought the Gronowalskis to Walter. But the big-city lawyers had been able to keep the case from coming to trial till now. "And you didn't tell me," Martha said.

Walter smiled, forgiving her for being too busy to listen. Seeing that smile, the kind curve of his lips, she felt the impact of him with a shock of newness—his patience, his strength, his utter steadfastness. She reached out a hand.

He drew her up to stand within his enclosing arms. She opened her lips upon his cheek, and at that moment he spoke against her hair: "It will be all right."

Her breath caught in something like a laugh. "That was just what I was telling you!"

Then he was gone and the door downstairs closed once more, softly this time. She sat before her cooling soup and remembered how Walter had waited this morning, waited for something she had not given him. "I need to carry my marriage with me," he had told her early in their first year, "through a day of people versus other people."

It had touched her deeply at the time, but that was before the children came, crowding between them, postponing their moments alone together until they were too exhausted—or she was. Like last night—she remembered how he had stood watching her press the ribbon, waiting for her to feel his need of her attention, of her whole self. He always liked to talk about his cases with her before he went into court. "If your wife can't find the holes in your argument," he had once said with a grin, "it's a sure bet no jury will." But once a trial had begun, he never could discuss it. She had let him down this time.

* * * * *

The doorbell rang and Dr. Joe came up the stairs. He nodded at her but saved his friendly smile for Philip. His words were gentle as he unbuttoned Phil's shirt and placed the stethoscope against his chest. His face was blank as he listened, but when he laid the boy back on the pillow he said casually, "Looks like the real thing. 'Old-fashioned pneumonia.'"

Martha gasped, childhood whispers assailing her: ". . . reached the crisis . . . failed to rally . . ."

"Of course, that's easier to deal with nowadays," Dr. Joe went on, "than the new-fashioned virus kind. We can give miracle drugs and *get* miracles usually." He was writing on his prescription pad. "I'll phone Ed Robbins, and he'll drive right over with the penicillin. If the case is typical, that temperature should do a rather spectacular dive."

After he had phoned he came partway back up the stairs. "He'll need pretty constant nursing care, you know, to keep him quiet after the fever drops. But it's important. I could get him into the hospital at Marbury if you can't handle it."

"Of course I can," she told him.

"Good." He started down. "At that age a kid is better off in his own bed. Especially at Christmas."

Christmas . . . the word echoed back to her when he had gone. Was it still the nineteenth of December?

She had never liked the local druggist, Ed Robbins—his familiar manner repelled her—but when he came bursting into the house within ten minutes, she could not speak for gratitude. "If you need anything else, just give me a buzz," he grunted. "Hot-water bottle, ice bag, anything, if I have to go to Marbury for it."

The tears must have been near the surface, for they spilled over. "Oh, thanks, Ed."

He was gone and she was tearing the package open, rousing Philip. He took his first capsule with unlikely meekness, sinking back to the pillow in relief. There was no difficulty

now, she thought grimly, in keeping him quiet. No, this was the time to finish what she could of those tasks that had been so pressing this morning. If she could only think what they were. But anxiety was like a thick fog filling her mind.

* * * * *

The sound of Sandy's feet on the porch was infinitely welcome. "Can I come up?" he stage-whispered.

From the doorway she nodded. His feet clumped carefully on the stairs; total willpower could not keep those shoes really quiet. He gazed down at his little brother, his teeth biting into his lower lip. She noted how like his father's his gray eyes were, with their thick, dark lashes, the brows slashed blackly across the level forehead. Even his jaw was losing its curve and beginning to thrust out ruggedly like Walter's, daring anyone to misinterpret the dimple in the chin. "Phil looks so . . . sick," he whispered.

"He's had his first penicillin. There must be quite a battle starting in him. But soon he'll be needing a nurse to hold him down."

Sandy's eyes went to hers in alarm.

"I'll be the nurse." She smiled.

"Gads!" Sandy wiped his forehead. It was one of his histrionic gestures, but this time it looked real. "You had me scared. We don't want any old Starch-face around. Not at Christmas."

There was that word again, that strange and meaningless word. But not meaningless to the children. They would still be expecting, anticipating. "Sandy, I'm afraid our Christmas this year—" She groped for words to soften the blow. "Well, this has caught me with some rather important unfinished—"

"Say, speaking of which!" And Sandy went clumping down the stairs.

Kids never heard what they didn't want to hear, she thought, sighing. If only she could be that way, if only she need not hear every hasty, painful breath Phil drew! They seemed faster, shallower, and he moved restlessly on the bed. He was gasping out incoherent words that terrified her. She sponged his body—how small he was!—and dressed him in clean pajamas, but he hardly noticed.

* * * * *

At last Walter came in. "I saw Sandy riding his bike through a foot of snow with a knapsack on his back, well filled. Is he off to Everest?"

"The packages!"

"The walks are cleared," Walter marveled. "Even the driveway."

"He did that at noon," Martha told him.

He took her hand, and their fingers communicated something comprehensible only to two people who had shared a two-year-old's tantrums, a six-year-old's attacks upon his sister, a ten-year-old sitter's desertion of his baby brother for a baseball game. But Sandy was thirteen now.

"That must be the zigzag course of growing up," Walter mused. "A matter of rising to occasions and then not slipping all the way back."

Philip had seemed quieter as they talked, but now he moved again. "It's nearly time for more penicillin," Martha said.

"It keeps going all night? Let's take turns."

She shook her head. "Remember Gronowalski versus Fullerton. How did it go?"

"Judge Gresham didn't seem bowled over by my opening."

"He just took pains to conceal it."

"Do you really think so?" Walter gave a good imitation of a grin. He stood. "I'll bring up the garden chaise. You can rest on it daytimes during his convalescence."

Wonderful word, she thought. But Walter was only whistling in the dark, playing a game of make-believe, pretending the agonizing doubt was all behind them.

Prilly was home, helping him bring the chaise lounge up the stairs. "Elspeth's mother came to help decorate," she chattered. "And she's going to make my costume along with Elspeth's."

"How lovely of her!" Martha had forgotten all about the costume. She must pull herself together. "If one of you will stay up here, I'll get supper."

Prilly seized her arms and pushed her awkwardly down on the chaise. "Promise you won't come *near* the kitchen till I say you can." Her slim body was rigid with intensity.

"You know how much trouble a nurse can make among the help," Walter added.

Prilly did not smile. Reigning in the kitchen had always been her dream. Martha wondered how she could have denied the boon because of anything so trivial as cleaning counters, walls, and floor. "I promise," she said. This was one gift, at least, that she could give the child.

The doorbell rang as Philip took his second capsule. From her separate, remote world upstairs Martha was aware of Mrs. Carhart's voice spraying like a fountain over Walter's low tones. But all she really heard was Philip's hasty, urgent breathing.

Walter brought her supper tray. She stared at crusty chicken pie, breathed the fragrant steam. "Mrs. Carhart brought it," Walter explained. "With good news. It seems everybody in town bought one another's cakes at fancy prices."

Martha tried to laugh, but the tears were too near the surface. Mrs. Carhart had been so petulant only six hours ago. Six hours? Six decades.

* * * * *

It seemed that the doorbell rang all evening long. The news had swept through the small town, bringing gifts and offers. *But this meant Philip's case was more serious than she had been told,* Martha thought in panic. No, Dr. Joe would never reveal any worry he felt. He would not need to; the word was enough—pneumonia.

It was after the doorbell and the phone were still, the children asleep and Walter reluctantly gone to bed—it was then that the horror started.

She looked at Philip lying quiet in his bed, quiet but for his rapid breathing, his body small beneath the covers, extending little more than halfway down the bed. Watching a five-year-old run about all day, shouting and climbing, you forget how tenuous is the hold by which a child that age clings to life.

She began to hear what Dr. Joe had really said, what she had not let herself hear when he said it. "We can get a miracle usually." *Usually.* It was like a hanging sword ready to cut off hope.

"If this case is typical . . ." *If.*

But suppose it was not. The whispers she had overheard as a child came hissing in her ears: ". . . reached the crisis . . . failed to rally . . . reached the crisis. . ."

She fought the impulse to call Dr. Joe. "Phone me if you

have any questions," he had said. Well, she had a question for him. Just one—whether her son, her baby, would live or die.

But asking the doctor would not change the answer. There was nothing for her to do now but wait. Nothing, no work for her speeding, efficient hands. No plans to fill the mind that had teemed with lists and schedules. Nothing but thoughts of how those busy hands, that busy mind, had failed her husband and her son.

At last she could give Philip another capsule. She set the alarm clock again, placed it under her pillow, and lay back on the chaise. She had not known how tired she was. She closed her aching eyes. Without losing awareness of Philip's breathing she began to dream. She was watching in fascination a broad, red satin ribbon, creased and wrinkled like a prehistoric reptile; watching in sick horror she saw it writhe and change, become sleek and shiny, like the stretched skin of some naked, snakelike animal, writhing, changing again to creases . . . wrinkles . . . She started up, her temples wet and cold, her heart racing with fear. She dared not doze again, but her waking thoughts were worse.

At three in the morning, when she knew that she had not only blighted her husband's life but sacrificed his son's, she heard Walter's step in the hall.

She went to him and pressed her shivering body close to his. "Couldn't you sleep?" she whispered.

"Not without you . . ." He held her closer. "Listen."

She stood very still. She could hardly hear Philip's breathing. It was quieter now and slower, definitely slower. She moved swiftly to lay her hand on his forehead. The skin was warm and faintly damp, as a sleeping child's should be. Her eyes met Walter's just as her knees gave way. She would have fallen but for his arm half carrying her to the chaise. He knelt beside her, his cheek against her hair. "You'll sleep now." He kissed her lips.

"You too," she murmured, and was asleep.

The alarm clock buzzed under her pillow. She sat up and blinked in the faint dawn light. But even before she was awake she heard the slow, steady rhythm of Philip's breathing. His eyes were closed, really closed, no sightless gleam between the lids; his lashes lay golden on his cheek.

She wakened him to take his capsule. This time he looked into her face. "Mommy." It was a greeting, the greeting of someone who has been away and has come back.

"Hi, Phil." She kept her arms from clutching him to her breast. "Another capsule for you. Down with it."

He stared at it, frowning in natural suspicion, all meekness gone. "Is it good?"

"Good?" She laughed. "It's wonderful."

He looked a little puzzled, but he took it with a wry, resigned half smile, so familiar, so dear, so much himself, her Phil, that she felt the impulse to run wildly down the hall opening doors, shouting the news.

He looked at the chaise. "Why are you sleeping here? Have we got company?"

"You have," she told him. "And I'm it."

His smile became a wide, delighted grin. "Truly?"

"Truly."

He reached his hand out and she held it: little and thin but no longer limp—very much alive.

The gray sky was lightening beyond the window; a flush of color warmed the east.

"Is that the sunrise?" Philip asked. "It's pretty."

"Very pretty. Shall we go back to sleep?"

He shook his head contentedly. "No. Let's talk about the sunrise."

They did not speak often, though. They lay against their pillows watching the light rise through the ragged purple clouds.

Soon they saw that the air was full of snow, large flakes drifting lazily or swirling upward in foolish whirlwinds before they settled slowly to the earth. Once, seeing a particularly frivolous burst of snowflakes, they both laughed aloud, and Philip said, "I like having company."

She was abashed suddenly before the light in his eyes, the calm serenity, the joy. It was so little she had done for him, just sitting with him, just watching snowflakes, just being with him. Yet she could not remember another time when she had simply shared time with a child, doing nothing, striving for nothing, giving nothing—nothing but herself. Nor could she remember feeling for years this strange tranquility in which she rested now.

* * * * *

The alarm clock buzzed; she offered him another capsule. He swallowed and informed her, "It stinks."

"We don't say that in *this* house," Prilly crowed in the doorway, her eyebrows raised in triumphant question.

Martha nodded as she placed the thermometer firmly beneath Philip's tongue and closed his lips with her fingers.

Sandy came stumbling out of his room. "What gives?" He yawned, but his gray eyes shone brilliantly upon his brother.

"Oh, nothing," Prilly told him in her usual teasing voice. "Nothing but everything."

"His temperature is almost normal," Martha said, and had to add, "Hush—you'll wake your father."

"Father is waked, completing the family group." Walter stood grinning and posed with a hand on each older child's shoulder.

Philip studied the picture a moment. "Merry Christmas," he said.

Sandy and Prilly protested; it was not the right moment. Christmas was five days off. But Martha looked over their heads at their father. Philip was right. This *was* the moment, Christmas *would* be merry. For the first time it would be really right, and the rightness had already begun. The ritual might be made up of makeshift parts, many tasks might be performed imperfectly or left undone, the most important presents not wrapped up or even purchased, but none of those given would be without the giver.

In his convalescence Phil might be fretful. Sandy and Prilly might slip from the giddy pinnacle of their new maturity. But this night was forever theirs, their family treasure—their miracle.

She felt tears come to her eyes and looked across at Walter. It was almost as if he thought what she was thinking, for his gray eyes were lustrous, dark. In that moment of quiet, it was almost as though she could hear music swell and fill the room: *"How silently, how silently, the wondrous gift is given!"*

Hope Hale Davis (1903–2004), born in Iowa City, Iowa, held many positions in her long life, and was a prolific writer of short stories for magazines such as *Colliers, New Yorker, Bookman, Redbook,* and *Town and Country.*

Christmas on the Mayflower

Elizabeth Cady Stanton

Have you ever wondered if those ultraconservative Pilgrims dared to celebrate Christmas on that landing day, December 25, of 1620?

Wonder no longer!

* * * * *

This would be a great story for children to act out at Christmas.

* * * * *

Historians take so little note of the doings of women and children that I presume not one of my readers ever heard of Christmas on the *Mayflower*; and yet the unwritten history of individuals and nations is always most interesting. I am indebted for my facts to Elizabeth Tudor Brewster, named after the queen. She was a favorite niece of Elder William Brewster, who went to Holland with the Pilgrims and lived there several years. My husband's mother was a Brewster, and into her hands came many of the private family letters, dim and yellow with time, and among others this account of Christmas.

While yet at sea, the mothers began to discuss the probabilities of reaching land by December 25, and having some little celebration for the children, as they had half a dozen on board of the right age to enjoy some holiday performances. The foremothers who came from Holland had imbibed the Dutch love for festive occasions, and were more liberal in their views than the rigid Puritans direct from England, who objected to all the legends of old Saint Nicholas. But Elder Brewster, then seventy-nine years old, and loving children tenderly, gave his vote for the celebration.

Accordingly, as they sailed up the beautiful harbor of Plymouth, the mothers were busy in their preparations for the glad day. Knowing the fondness of Indians for beads, they had brought a large box of all sizes and colors, which they were stringing for the little Indians, as they intended to invite a few of them to come on board the ship. The mothers had also brought a barrel full of ivy, holly, laurel, and immortelles,* to decorate their log cabins. Of these they made wreaths to ornament the children and the saloon.†

As soon as the *Mayflower* cast anchor, Elder Brewster and his interpreter, and as many of the fathers and mothers as the little boats would hold, went ashore to make arrangements for their cabins, to visit the squaws and invite the children. The interpreter explained to them the meaning or significance of Christmas, the custom of exchanging gifts and so forth, and they readily accepted the invitation. Massasoit was sachem [chief] of the Wampanoags at this point. The yellow fever had reduced his tribe, once estimated at thirty thousand, down to

---

* Everlasting plants.

† Dining cabin on a ship.

three hundred, now scattered all along the southern coast of Massachusetts.

When the Pilgrims landed, there were only a few huts at that point. But the noble chief Massasoit was there, fortunately for our little colony, consisting only of one hundred and two, all told—men, women, and children. Massasoit was a splendid specimen of manhood, honest, benevolent, and he loved peace.

When Christmas dawned, bright and beautiful, he came on board with two squaws and six little boys and girls, all in their ornaments, paint, and feathers, the children in bright scarlet blankets, and caps made of white rabbit-skins, the little ears standing up on their foreheads, and squirrel tails hanging down their backs. Each one carried a small basket containing beech- and hickory-nuts and wintergreen berries, which they presented gracefully to the English children standing in a line ready to receive them.

The interpreter had taught them to say "Happy to see you," "Welcome," and "Farewell" in the Indian tongues. So they shook hands and received the natives graciously, presenting them, in turn, with little tin pails filled with fried cakes, almonds and raisins, some bright English pennies, a horn, and a drum. The mothers tied strings of beads around their necks, wrists, and ankles, with which they were greatly pleased.

They went all over the ship and asked many questions about all they saw. When Massasoit

proposed to go, the mothers urged him to stay to dinner; but he declined, saying that they did not understand English customs in eating and that the children would not know how to use knives, forks, and spoons.

Moreover, he said they never ate except when they were hungry, and the sun was still too high for that.

The exchanging of presents was a very pretty ceremony, and when they were ready to depart, the good elder placed his hands on each little head, giving a short prayer and his blessing. While all this was transpiring, the squaws asked the foremothers to give them beads, which they readily did, and placed wreaths of ivy on their heads. As they paddled away in their little canoes, the horns and drums sounded.

Then the mothers decorated their tables and spread out a grand Christmas dinner. Among other things, they brought a box of plum-puddings. It is an English custom to make a large number of plum-puddings at Christmastime and shut them up tight in small tin pails and hang them on hooks on the kitchen wall, where they keep for months. You see them in English kitchens to this day. With their plum-puddings, gooseberry tarts, Brussels sprouts, salt fish, and bacon, the Pilgrims had quite a sumptuous dinner. Then they sang "God Save the King" and went on deck to watch the sun go down and the moon rise in all her glory.

The children took their little baskets to their berths, the last objects of interest on which their eyes rested as they fell asleep.

Elizabeth Cady Stanton (1815–1901) was the nineteenth century's most prominent proponent of women's legal and social equality. In 1848, she and others organized the first national woman's rights convention in Seneca Falls, New York. In 1851, she met Susan B. Anthony, and their remarkable collaboration changed history. After the Civil War, she was one of the best-known and most highly esteemed women in the United States.

Home, Sweet Home

Malone Hobson

This Christmas, Marty Anne Houston declared she was going to run away from the old women's home.

And run away she did! Run away to the home where she and her husband had been so happy.

But when she got there—

* * * * *

This 97-year-old story deserves to live again. Not least because our age tends to thoughtlessly assume that mere retirement housing is a valid substitute for love, cherishing, and personal tender care

* * * * *

The sun has so much shine in it this morning it makes one think of bees and singing brooks and roses and Christmas gifts!"

Blithe as a robin's call was a voice from the low chair under the great moss-draped live oak. A sunbeam danced through the swaying leaves and, touching two old heads, it turned their dull gray to shining silver. At the same moment two pairs of dim eyes glanced toward the occupant of the low chair, while two members of the inmost social circle of the Norwood Retreat for Aged Gentlewomen quivered with excitement.

"Mary Annie Houston, are you going to run away this Christmas?" Mrs. Wilmot leaned from her wheelchair at a dangerous angle to whisper the question.

"I am!" Little Mrs. Houston spoke with a decision that was as surprising as if a dove should stamp its foot.

"Three years I fought that longing to go back home Christmas, and three times my heart outpulled my will, and I gave in. This time I shall not waste a single minute struggling with the longing! This Christmas I shall go—home."

"Sometimes I wish I had the courage to go with you." Miss Matilda White gave a genteel sigh and stroked her left cheek tenderly. "But with my sensitive wisdom tooth I have to be very careful."

"I wish *I* had the courage and the strength to start off alone, like Mary Annie," Mrs. Wilton moaned dismally, and straightened her gay shawl across her knees. "I just sit here as if my whole business in life was to think about the sciatica in my leg. And I am only sixty-nine and Mary Annie is past seventy!"

"Seventy-six last July," amended Miss Matilda, who knew the birthdays and the ages of all her associates at the refuge.

"Both of you hold so tight to your special moans, you haven't time to catch your joys as they go by. *I* turn my worries and my aches loose!" Mrs. Houston laughed as blithely as a girl. "Daniel used to say I shed troubles exactly as a chicken does its feathers."

"I wish *I* could!" Mrs. Wilton sighed. "And tomorrow is Christmas Eve too! But I like a *white* Christmas. Fruit and flowers in the garden don't seem right at this season."

"I'm from New England and I love a Christmas that's cold, with roaring fires and sleigh bells," murmured Miss Matilda.

"I don't!" Mrs. Houston announced. "Seems to me that when the Christ Child came to earth He brought rare gifts from Paradise with Him, and they must have been warm, beautiful things, like the lovely flowers and fruits and—"

"*Birds!*" chirped Miss Matilda with unexpected briskness. "Among His gifts there must have been lovely birds, Mary Annie."

"*One* bird, Matilda," Mrs. Houston's soft voice crooned. "The mockingbird could sing all the other birds' songs for Him."

Three pairs of weary old eyes grew introspective. The pages of the years were turned back until each found the Christmas picture of her young time.

* * * * *

Christmas Eve morning the atmosphere of the Norwood Retreat was charged with excitement, all the deeper because it was so quiet.

Mrs. Houston's place was vacant at breakfast. The immediate effect of her absence was astonishing. Feebleness fell from the old ladies like garments cast aside. Miss Matilda propelled Mrs. Wilmot's wheelchair so vigorously through the front door that it skidded gaily down the steps, turned turtle, and nearly smothered its occupant among her own silk cushions.

With one accord the old ladies flocked down the path and across the tiny lawn to the shade beneath the giant live oak. This spot was sacred to the three who formed the inmost social circle of the Norwood Retreat. But that morning all social rules were recklessly broke.

"To think of her being out all alone!" As she turned to Miss Clayton, the nurse, there was an anxious pucker between the matron's eyes. "Mrs. Houston is almost eighty, and she knows no more about the world than a baby!"

"She'll come back safe." A low laugh of tender amusement came from Miss Clayton's lips. "This makes the fourth Christmas Eve she has run away. Once a big policeman brought her and a bag of peanuts home in a taxi."

"It's heartbreaking!" the matron gulped. "Whenever she runs away, she starts out toward her old home where she and her husband owned a little orange grove. Our old ladies get on all right through the year, but when Christmas comes, all hearts sing just one song, and that is 'Home, Sweet home!'"

* * * * *

In her tight gray bonnet and gray gown, Mrs. Houston might have been a bit of drifting cloud as she walked briskly along the white shell road, sheltered from the morning sun by the huge leaves of the palmettos that grew on either side.

"The Christmas glory is shining everywhere!" Mary Annie murmured contentedly to herself as she sat down under a giant pine to rest. She turned her pretty little silver head on one side and looked critically at her shoe.

"Seems like the Christmas giving is actually in my feet!" She laughed aloud joyously at her own quaint conceit. "And it is making them very strong to bear me—home." After a few moments, she was on her way again, walking with the steady, purposeful steps of a young woman.

After three, for the first time that day Mary Annie's blithely tripping feet lagged.

"It's right down that cross lane," she faltered, "my home where I lived for forty years with Daniel." She paused when she reached the turn.

"I've never come this near it since it was sold," she said aloud. "Each time I started to come, something turned me back to the institution. But today it seems as if something high and holy was singing in my heart, urging me to go right on—home!"

The small, crumpled rose-leaf face quivered, but the little feet stepped bravely along the lane that led to a lawn. When she came to the white gate, Mary Annie stood looking as one looks who drinks with her eyes.

"It seems as if I can't be awake and seeing all this!" she faltered. "Why, the house, and the roses and the orange trees—why, they are Daniel's and my home dream come true!"

Mary Annie entered the gate and tip-toed up the walk between the blooming roses, toward the seemingly empty house. As she neared the veranda she paused, her attention caught by the sound of a busy hoe. A mockingbird poured forth a song of glory from the top of a lofty pine.

"It sounds like our own bird, the very one that sang for Daniel and me on our wedding day."

"Chris'mas gif', Lady!" She turned hastily and met the smile of an aged man who had approached from around the house, with a hoe on his shoulder.

"Why—Christmas gift, Uncle!" She managed to smile as she returned the old Southern holiday greeting.

"You looks nigh petered out, ma'am. Come right up on the veranda and res' yo'self." Then, as she hesitated, he added, "Me and Mr. Ludlow we got here yesterday, to spend the Chris'mus. He'll be pintedly pleased to have you come in an' set a spell."

"I lived here a long time ago," Mary Annie said as she

mounted the steps slowly. "I—came in—because it seemed like—home."

"What is it, Uncle Alec?" A tall young man stepped out on the veranda.

* * * * *

"Come in, will you not?" he invited, smiling down into the delicate face that was smiling up at him. "You can't imagine how glad I shall be to have a Christmas guest."

"And you can't imagine how much I feel like part of a fairy tale come true!" Mary Annie faltered, as she sank into the big easy chair. Persian rugs covered the floor; rare pictures were on the walls; an old mahogany highboy filled the corner of the south window; the very chair she was sitting in would have made a collector break the tenth commandment.

"You used to live here?" His words brought Mary Annie back from the past with a little jump.

"Oh, *so* long ago!" she faltered. "It was our first home, Daniel's and mine."

"I wish you would tell me about it." He made the request boyishly. For the first time she noticed how young he was—not more than twenty-two or three, she thought. And then, in response to the genuine interest in his eyes, she told him about her life, bit by bit.

"Daniel and I were married on Christmas Eve." She did not mind if he saw the tear that slipped down her cheek.

"My wife and I came here last Christmas Eve on our honeymoon. I bought this little place and furnished it, for her," he said, as the boyish smile vanished.

"You will tell me about her?" the gentle old voice asked.

"We—quarreled last Easter in Richmond, and—she left me." The question was answered as simply as it had been asked.

"Yes?" There was a longing to help in Mary Annie's question.

"We were both hot-tempered, and I said hard, unkind, untrue things to her. She was such a proud little creature! I don't blame her a bit." He paused.

"And you just had to come home for Christmas." Mary Annie's voice was saturated with understanding. He nodded and walked over to the window.

* * * * *

"You see, neither of us had any people. There were just the two of us. And—I don't know where she is! I wrote to her in care of everyone I knew, but there has never been a word since she went away. She had money of her own, and she drew a lot out of the bank the day she left—but the bank has not heard from her since.

"I thought maybe I wouldn't be so lonely here as I was in the house in Richmond, but it's ten times worse! For it was here we were so happy, and I seem to see her and hear her all over the place! We stood at this very window last Christmas Eve, listening to the mockingbird. He seemed to be welcoming us—home." After a pause he added huskily, "I wish you'd stay. I can't stand tomorrow here alone."

Would she stay? Pink cheeks and radiant eyes gave her answer before her fingers began removing the little gray bonnet.

"And we'll have a tree, my dear!" Mary Annie quivered, patting her silver curls. "A real, piney Christmas tree?"

"We will!" The flush on his cheeks and the sparkle in his eyes made him look very boyish, she noted with a sigh of satisfaction. "As soon as I get the Norwood, and fix it so they can't take you away from me, I'll go over beyond the grove where the pines grow thick, and I'll cut the very prettiest Christmas tree I can find!"

"Glory!" sang out Uncle Alec. "A Christmas tree! Praise God! I'm beginning to feel the Christmas spirit deep in my old bones. Just wait until I get my basket and shears and I'll head over to the grove and pick the biggest Tasselberry oranges I can find. Then I'll make tracks to Sister Judy Ann Tasselberry and buy the fattest gobbler in her yard! And, God-willing, when tomorrow comes, I'll cook just as good a dinner as I cooked last Christmas when our little Missy was here with her shining eyes and golden head!"

* * * * *

So it came about that Mary Annie was all alone in the bungalow an hour later. She had placed roses in the rooms, and following the dictates of her own heart, she had filled a silver bowl with glowing red beauties in the room she felt had belonged to the little Christmas bride of a year ago. Then she went out and sat down on the top step of the front veranda, under the shadow of a big wild jessamine vine.

"Seems as if we are Christmas gifts, sent to each other by the Christ Child," she mused, looking at the flower garden through happy eyes. So lost was she in plans for the Christmas tree that Jack was to bring, that she did not hear an approaching taxi until it stopped at the white gate in the oleander hedge....

A slim girlish figure then stepped down, bearing a pink bundle in her arms.

"The blessed Christ Child has sent the boy two precious gifts!" As she rose to greet the newcomer, Mary Annie's heart sang a Te Deum.

* * * * *

"And Jack doesn't know about his little boy?" Half an hour later Mary Annie was back in her position on the front veranda step. Across her lap lay the pink bundle. It had been opened, revealing a tiny head covered with golden down. A wee hand lay on a fold of the pink blanket like a stray rose petal. In a low wicker chair, drawn very close to Mary Annie and the pink bundle, sat a slim little figure in a blue gown.

"I didn't know about our little boy when I—left Jack." The golden head bent for a moment over the pink bundle. "I didn't like children—then."

"I have always been so glad Mary of Nazareth loved little children," Mary Annie said reflectively. "If Mary hadn't loved them, she would not have given the world its first great Christmas Gift."

"I know, now." The sweet young voice spoke steadily, and in its low undertone was the note that only a mother's love can give. The lovely shining head drooped until it was very close to the silver one.

"It was—my love for the baby that made me come back to Jack. It made me know what real love is. We had quarreled, you know, so bitterly. We had said such hard things to each other, things I did not think either of us could ever forgive. Then—after the baby came I knew that love means suffering and forgiveness—and—"

"Forgetting," Mary Annie's soft voice interrupted. "Dear heart, it means the letting go; the turning loose forever of even the memory of the things that have hurt. Why, once Daniel said I was a feather-headed minx, and I called him a brute and threatened to go home to my mother! Years later we laughed

together about it, because—" The star-bright old eyes, filled with laughter, looked into two big, inquiring, blue eyes.

"Because?" prompted the girl, in deeply interested tones.

"Why, dear child, we had both forgotten what that wonderful quarrel was about!" Mary Annie's delighted laughter bubbled forth joyously, and the young, sweet ringing laugh mingled deliciously with that of the older woman.

The joyous duet fell upon the ears of a tall young man, who was turning the corner of the house, with a brave Christmas tree on his shoulder. He paused at the veranda, his face white.

"Jack!" The girl was on her feet and down the steps like a flash of light.

"Claire!" A new heaven and a new earth opened before his eyes as he held out his arms and clasped his wife to him.

* * * * *

It was late afternoon the day after Christmas that a big, high-powered car stopped before the entrance to the Norwood Refuge for Aged Gentlewomen. It gave many prosperous snorts and gurgles while Mary Annie Houston alighted, helped carefully by a tall, handsome young man, who stood, hat in hand, while he opened and closed the gate for her.

Every old lady in the house was watching. They all saw the beautiful girlish face that leaned out of the car, while a little gloved hand waved farewell.

"Everything was lovely, like a dream come true," Mary Annie confided to Miss Matilda and Mrs. Wilmot that night in her room.

"And where had she been?" asked Mrs. Wilmot.

"With an old teacher of hers in New York, someone that Jack never knew. Her baby was born there, and when she was well enough to travel she went to the home in Richmond. He wasn't there, and her heart told her she would find him keeping Christmas here where they had come on their honeymoon."

"And their little child is a boy." Mrs. Wilmot's eyes were soft and brooding, as a woman's eyes are when she looks at a baby through dreams of its future.

"They have everything but kin," said Mary Annie contentedly. "I am to go out there next week to stay and be a grandma."

"I feel like a great-aunt to them, knowing *you* so well, Mary Annie." Mrs. Wilmot's voice had a little break in it.

"*I* don't!" declared Matilda recklessly, as she rose and grasped Mrs. Wilmot's wheelchair to push it from the room. "I feel like a real grandma to that little Christmas child, even if I haven't seen it."

Mary Annie's glance went from one old face to the other. She smiled softly.

"They are both very young, and full of wanting to pass on to others the sort of gifts the Christ Child brought to earth, love and kindness and peace and goodwill," she said. "And Claire says that when heart-spreading days come, like Christmas, they'll need all of us out there for real kin." And in Mary Annie's radiant smile there lay the promise of new joys dawning for Norwood's little family.

Malone Hobson wrote for popular magazines early in the twentieth century.

We Two, Together

Mary Russell

Christmas alone—Marjorie was near tears. What on earth was there to look forward to now?

But then something happened to take her mind off her troubles: Mrs. Esmont's were so much worse!

* * * * *

"What are you doing for Christmas, Marjorie?" Janet Towner called across the space that separated their desks.

"Nothing."

"What do you mean, 'nothing'?"

"I have no one to make Christmas with. No one belongs to me, so, I'm going to forget that tonight is Christmas Eve and that tomorrow is Christmas."

"But you can't do that," Janet protested.

"Oh, yes, I can!" The strained note in Marjorie's voice belied her gaiety. "I'm going to take five books from the library, lock myself in my room tonight, and tomorrow read until the day is gone."

"You'll do no such thing! You'll come home with me. I'd love to have you."

"Thanks, but I couldn't do that—go into somebody else's home. You have to have your own Christmas."

"How about spending the evening with me?" Bill Ames asked as he sauntered across the office to Marjorie's desk. "This is my first Christmas away from home, and I'll admit I feel sort of lost. Kind of homesick, I guess." He grinned at Marjorie in a sort of boyish fashion and asked, "What do you say? Shall we be miserable together?"

Marjorie did not know what to say. Any other time she would have been delighted with an invitation from Bill. He was good-looking, tall, athletic in build. His black hair was wavy. His eyes, on occasion, danced with humor. However, it was not only his looks that appealed to her, but his frank face, his sincere, fearless manner, his friendly attitude toward everyone. Ever since she had come to the office to work four weeks before, she had hoped that she and Bill might become friends.

But she could not go out with him this Christmas Eve, when she was so miserable and unhappy. Yet, if she refused, he might never ask her again.

Before she could frame a reply, Janet spoke. "You'll both come home with me. After dinner we'll go caroling with a group of young people from our church. You'll like them."

"Great!" Bill was enthusiastic. "At home we always went caroling on Christmas Eve. What do you say, Marjorie?"

Marjorie shook her head. "I'm afraid that pretending I'm having a good time won't do any good in my case. But you go, Bill. Please don't mind about me."

"I'll do no such thing. You'll spend the evening with me."

"But—"

"But you shall," Bill interrupted. "You're not going to spend Christmas Eve alone in your room. Chances are you'd be crying instead of reading. We'll have dinner at a nice little place I know, where they serve real home cooking. Then we'll drive around and see the crowds and the decorations."

Marjorie still meant to refuse, but before she dared trust her voice, Bill was swinging across the room. At the door he turned and called back, with his friendly smile, "I'll be seeing you—about seven." Then he was gone.

At seven Marjorie was ready. She looked very sweet and lovely, even with the sadness that overshadowed her face, for her soft green crepe brought out the golden glints in her hair, and accentuated the fairness of her skin. In spite of herself, she experienced a little thrill of anticipation as she took her coat from its hanger, her gloves and purse from the drawer.

Seven-fifteen came—seven-thirty—seven-fifty, but no Bill. Wasn't he coming? Then the doorbell rang jut as the clock was striking eight.

"Sorry to be late," Bill apologized, "but I was detained." And that was all the explanation he offered.

In the car, driving toward town, Marjorie tried to make conversation, but Bill did not help her much. He answered her mostly in short sentences and made no comments of his own. Soon Marjorie became silent, thinking that perhaps Bill wished to give all his attention to the heavy traffic, made more hazardous than usual by excited hurrying pedestrians who paid little heed to signals. But when they had reached a less traveled highway, Bill was still quiet and preoccupied.

"Are you disappointed that we didn't go caroling?" Marjorie asked.

"Caroling?" he repeated, puzzled.

"With Janet's crowd."

"Oh, that! I'd forgotten. It would have been pleasant, but I like this quite as well."

"Bill, what's the matter?"

"Nothing. That is, nothing with me, or us."

"But something is troubling you. Can't you tell me?"

"It's Mrs. Esmont where I live. I stopped in just now to leave her a box of candy and found her crying because she had not been able to do anything for the children for Christmas. She has had flu, been sitting up only a few days. I feel sorry for the youngsters. Pretty tough to be a kid and have no Christmas."

"How old are they?"

"Oh, Teddy is about five, and Nancy's around seven, I guess. Awfully cute, both of them."

"Did—did you do anything?"

"I sent them a dinner, but that won't help much. I don't believe Mrs. Esmont is able to cook it."

"Isn't there anyone to cook it for her?"

"Don't think so. She had a woman for awhile, but as soon as she began to gain she let her go. She has to count the pennies, I guess. Her husband died last spring. But it's the children I'm thinking of. They won't have much of a Christmas."

"Oh, yes, they will! We'll make it for them. Turn around and drive back to town."

"But you said—"

"Never mind what I said, do as I say now." She laughed a bit unsteadily.

As Bill swung the car about and headed back toward town, Marjorie asked, "What did you send?"

"A turkey, some potatoes, squash, onions, cranberries, and nuts. Not much of a dinner for an invalid, I'm afraid," he added with an apologetic laugh.

"But right for Christmas," she assured him. "If you'll stop at that market just ahead, I'll add a few things—some that will be better for the mother."

When they left the market, however, both were carrying packages. Bill had seen so many things he thought the family should have.

The last bundle having been stowed away in the back of the car, Marjorie said, "Now drive around the corner to that lot where they're selling Christmas trees."

"Marjorie!" Bill's voice rang with surprise and pleasure. "You're doing the whole thing for them!"

"*We* are," she laughed.

It took only a few minutes for Marjorie to find a tree that satisfied her, a well-shaped little fir with fragrant green branches.

"Now to the ten-cent store," she said as she snuggled down in the automobile seat, her hand still holding the little tree that she had insisted on keeping in front with her.

When the store had yielded up treasures of shining tinsel, glittering ornaments, toys, and small articles for stockings, Marjorie announced, "One more stop and we're through. We'll go into the department store next door, and while I'm buying a doll for Nancy, you select a train of cars for Teddy. It takes more than a dinner to make Christmas, especially for children." Then she added as an afterthought, "You can get the tree ready while I cook the dinner."

"Can you cook the turkey and all those

other things?" he asked in a voice tinged with doubt.

Marjorie laughed with amusement. "Can I? You wait and see."

It was an hour later that Bill unlocked the door of the house and ushered Marjorie into the house and into the living room. Three pairs of eyes turned and stared at Bill in amazement, at the tree on his back, at Marjorie with her arms filled with packages.

"Merry Christmas, everybody," Bill cried. "We've come to help you get ready for tomorrow. This is my friend, Marjorie Crandall, Mrs. Esmont."

He did not wait for Mrs. Esmont to speak. He knew she couldn't just then. Quickly he faced the children and asked, as he placed the tree on the floor, "Do you think you could help me trim this? We've got lots of pretty ornaments in some of these bundles." And he began to take packages from Marjorie.

With shouts of joy the children rushed at Bill, hands outstretched to receive packages. "Now, you open these while I carry the others to the kitchen," Bill told them. "I'll be back in a moment to help you."

It was perhaps an hour later that the loud cries of delight from the children brought Marjorie to the living room. There, filling a corner with brightness and fragrance, stood the little tree with its precious load of silver tinsel, colored glass ornaments, and tiny electric lights.

"It's perfectly lovely!" Marjorie exclaimed.

"Think so?" Bill asked as he swung around to face her.

He did not hear what she answered for he was gazing in astonishment at the girl. It was not the one he had seen at the office, not the girl with the sad stricken eyes, who seemed to have forgotten how to smile. The girl's eyes were shining with something more than excitement, and the radiance on her face surely came from within. He did not see that she was wearing one of Mrs. Esmont's house dresses, that her face was flushed with heat and unaccustomed exercise, that tiny ringlets had escaped from her waves. He knew only that she looked very attractive and that suddenly he felt a camaraderie with her that drove away the last remnant of his homesick feeling.

He flashed her a smile that quickened her pulse, then turned to Nancy who was pulling his sleeve and asking, "Is everything on?"

"Everything but the presents, and those never come until little girls and boys are in bed and asleep."

Nancy was silent a moment, then in a serious tone, she said, "Perhaps Teddy and I better be going now."

"You dear!" Marjorie exclaimed as she knelt and gathered the little girl in her arms. "I'll put you and Teddy to bed. After you're all snugly in, I'll tell you a story."

"Oh, goody, goody," came from both children as they scampered away into the next room.

Bill and Mrs. Esmont smiled at each other when they were alone, and each knew that the other was thinking of the girl who had followed the children. They sat, quietly listening, as her voice drifted out to them in the words of the beautiful old Christmas story.

When Marjorie began to sing, "Silent Night, Holy Night," Bill rose and tiptoed across the floor to peep in at the open door. A moment later, he recrossed the room, slipped an arm about Mrs. Esmont and guided her to the door. Unnoticed they watched the scene before them. Sitting in a little white

chair, between the two little beds was Marjorie, a hand held by each child. Nancy, who knew the words of the hymn, was singing with all her might, while Teddy, not to be left out, hummed the tune or made up words of his own.

Bill's rich baritone joined Marjorie's soprano on the second stanza. Mrs. Esmont added her sweet quavering voice. So they sang until they reached the last line, when all five, even Teddy, came out loud and clear in the words, "Christ the Savior is born."

There was still much to be done before Marjorie was ready to leave the house with its sleeping children, its grateful mother, its glistening tree, its partially cooked dinner. At last, she went to say good-bye to Mrs. Esmont.

"There is not one thing for you to do," she said. "I'll be over early to finish cooking the dinner."

"And will you stay and share it with us?" Something in Mrs. Esmont's voice made Marjorie think of her own mother, made her drop a kiss on the thin cheek before she answered, "I'd rather do that than anything else."

Then she and Bill were in the car, driving through the clear still night. Both were silent, thinking of another starlit night, of shepherds on a lonely hillside. As if to remind them of the angels' song, came the voices of carolers singing, "Joy to the world, the Lord is come."

As Bill left Marjorie at her house, he said, "I've made a discovery tonight, Marjorie. You don't need to be at home with your own family in order to find Christmas joy."

"I know," she said in a low voice, but one that held no hint of sorrow. "You can have it wherever you are—if you will."

From far off across the town a clock began to chime the hour of midnight. With shining eyes Bill and Marjorie faced each other, counting. On the stroke of twelve they cried as in one voice, "Merry Christmas!" Then Bill was gone with the promise to return early in the morning.

From the window of her room, Marjorie looked up into the starry heavens and softly repeated the song of the carolers, happy in her knowledge that He had come, and that she need never be lonely or without friends if she would but remember.

Mary Russell wrote for Christian magazines during the first half of the twentieth century.

The Red Glass Bowl

Margaret Weymouth Jackson

We are so spoiled with affluence today, so used to credit-card buying, that we've all but lost the element of sacrifice in our Christmas giving.

Five little children, all longing to give their mother a wonderful Christmas present—but how could they, with only eleven cents to spend? And the Great Depression of the 1930's raging.

* * * * *

As I re-read this remarkable story for the first time, I discovered, to my amazement, that the author had completely abandoned her usual writing style, making every sentence short, in words children could easily follow. Children will love this story, and beg their parents to read it out loud again and again!

* * * * *

No present ever held more real Christmas love than the red glass bowl.

* * * * *

The five little Andersons, with Peanut crowded close in among them, pressed their noses against the shining, plate-glass window of Mr. Phibbs's Cut-Price Jewelry Store and breathed as one. Their gaze was concentrated with a single intentness on the red glass bowl which stood on the second shelf of the window display. It was the most beautiful thing in the window, far lovelier than the rock-crystal goblets in sets, than the hand-painted cups and saucers, than the wrist watches and diamond rings, and strands of pearls and lesser jewels displayed cunningly. The bowl was about five inches across, deep garnet red in color, and with the most beautiful curlicues painted on it in gold. More precious than rubies, fairer than samite—and the price marked above it was only forty-nine cents, a great fortune to the five little Andersons, but cheap compared to other things in the window. Why, there was a diamond wristwatch priced at nineteen dollars in Mr. Phibbs's window!

Sis, the oldest, sighed profoundly. She was ten and wise in the ways of the street, and she knew that they must move on in a minute. Mr. Phibbs did not like children's noses pressed against his window, and the Anderson noses were well-known to all the shopkeepers in the neighborhood.

"If you all like it as much as I do, I'll talk to him," said Sis. "We've got eleven cents, between us."

The four little Andersons murmured ecstatically, and Peanut gave a yelp, his woolly, nondescript body quivering, his black eyes adoringly fixed on Sis' face.

"OK," said Sis, very business-like. "I'll go in alone. He wouldn't want us all in there. He's rich, Mr. Phibbs is, and that give him leave to holler. I'll give him the 'leven cents and ask him to keep it for us till Christmas. Then we can get the rest of the money and give it to Mummie for her present. Won't she be tickled?"

The four faces regarding her fixedly shone with pure joy. They all turned back again to look into the window.

"Now, Edith, you hold George's hand, and Maggie and Tillie, stand right together, and don't, on *no* account, go away from the window till I come out. Peanut, you stand right there, and don't you move!"

Peanut's stumpy tail vibrated, as the children grouped themselves obediently.

"And mind, now, if he'll keep it for us, don't ask Mummie for even one cent. It wouldn't be fair to get the money off her for her own Christmas present."

Sis paused at the door, gathering up her courage. Mr. Phibbs was really a terrible man, with his great gray and black beard and his shining bald head, and bushed eyebrows over eyes that looked more hard and shiny than anything in his store. Mr. Phibbs was known to be cross, and he was rich, which, in Sis's mind, added to his ogre-like qualities. Any little girl with eleven grimy pennies in her hand might well quail before him. But fear that some passing shopper would see the red glass bowl and instantly desire it goaded Sis to heroic effort. She opened the heavy door and went in, while Peanut and the children watched her with awe.

It was only half a store, half a number on the street. It ran back, long and narrow, a counter on one side, a wall on the other. In the back the big safe loomed. Behind the counter Mr. Phibbs towered, a giant in his black coat and beetling brows.

"Mr. Phibbs, please—"

"Sis Anderson, get those kids away from my window. I wash that window every day, and I want no sniveling—"

"Mr. Phibbs, please. We want to buy sumpin'."

Mr. Phibbs paused. She did not look as though she could buy much of anything, but you never could tell. You never could tell at all, Mr. Phibbs had learned.

"Mr. Phibbs, that red glass bowl in the window—we want it for Mummie, for Christmas. But we haven't got enough money."

"I couldn't mark it down another cent," said Mr. Phibbs instantly—almost, one might say, automatically. "It's already been marked down from a dollar. It's simulated cut glass. It's an imported piece. The gold on it is pure gold leaf."

"Oh, we wouldn't ask you to mark it down," protested Sis. "But we wanted to ask you to save it back for us."

"I couldn't do that either," said Mr. Phibbs. "There's half a dozen people want that bowl."

"Not for eleven cents deposit?" said Sis, torn between pride in the word and fear of Mr. Phibbs. "We got eleven cents, and we'll give it to you. We'll bring the rest of the money in as we get it. The other thirty-eight cents, I mean."

Mr. Phibbs paused. Eleven cents was eleven cents. He was no man to scorn a small sum. And the bowl was something no one else would think of buying.

"All right," he said, and was oddly startled at the glow in Sis' face, the epitome of rapture that lit it extravagantly. "But look here, now, Sis Anderson," he said sharply—he was a little confused by that pure Christmas light—"look here, now! If you don't bring in the money, you'll lose what you've paid. I can't hold that bowl and take a chance on not selling it, for nothing."

"Oh, no, Mr. Phibbs. We wouldn't want you to do that. We'll—we'll take a chance on the eleven cents."

Sis was actually pale at the thought of losing it, but one cannot get a mother a red glass bowl for Christmas without paying for it. She laid the pennies on the counter, and Mr. Phibbs picked them up and put them into his till quicker than magic.

Sis paused and began to leave, one foot at a time, reluctantly. "It's ten days to Christmas," she said. "We'll get it the day before Christmas, Mr. Phibbs."

"If you get some more money, you'd better bring it in here to me" he told her. "You might lose it."

She beamed at his kindness, and again he was astonished. She opened and closed the heavy door, and Peanut received her return with ecstasy worthy of an absence on a long journey.

The weather was mild, and the streets sloppy. Melting snow made a mess of the walks. Sis marshaled her family. George was short and fat. He was only two. Mother told Sis every day not to carry him, that he was too heavy for her, that he must learn to walk wherever they went. But Mother was no sooner out of sight than George got in front of Sis and hiked up his little leg.

"Dorge tired," he would say, and not budge another step.

Sis would lift him then, a staggering weight for her frail height, and lug him along with her. Edith, next to Sis, was eight, and the twins, Maggie and Tillie, were five, and then came ol' fat George, as the girls called him, following after his sisters, imposing on them, bossing them, to their hearts' complete content. It was the firm belief of the four little Anderson girls that George was the cutest baby in town. He was a darling, he was so sweet, and whenever he cried, they were all thrown into the most extreme sorrow and compassion, running eagerly to get what he liked, and doing all that they could do—and it was considerable—to appease hm.

Each school day Sis and Edith took the three little ones to the neighborhood free nursery before they went to school, but school was out until after New Year's, and Sis was in full charge.

All looked trustfully to her now, and all the little faces shone with the same rapture that had so oddly disturbed and upset Mr. Phibbs and made him sharper than usual, as Sis told them that Mr. Phibbs had taken the eleven cents and was going to keep the bowl for them until the day before Christmas. They looked once more, feeling entitled now, as cash customers, to look at the red glass bowl already practically their own.

Sis drew them gently away and got them started toward home. She carried George on her arm. Edith had a twin by each hand. Peanut brought up the rear, guarding them and herding them like the sheep dog he vaguely resembled, except for his small size. They strung along, looking greedily into windows, where toys abounded, where Christmas trees glittered, and papier maché characters smiled. The window of the cash-and-carry was a great pattern of apples and oranges, with nuts for trimming and holly wreaths laid over them. It was beautiful. Edith could scarcely bear to pass it, Sis admired it as an abstract phenomenon. Shoppers bustled the children. Peanut ran back and forth, barking and bouncing, airing derogatory opinions of every other dog on the street, and hastily retreating to Sis's feet when they returned his compliments.

They crossed a busy thoroughfare, bunched together for safety, turned down a block where the stores were poorer, and came to a narrow stairway that led up above a fur store to the loft overhead. Sis unlocked the door, after they had thumped up together, and Peanut crowded between their heels and was the first inside. The three rooms were surprisingly light and clean. Great windows on the street front towered above the store. Part of the day the sun peered into the big front room, and the two small rooms beyond. There were two beds in this front room, one for Sis and Edith, one for the twins. Mother slept in the small bedroom beside the kitchen, and she had a crib for George by her bed. There was no window in Mother's room. The kitchen was lighted from the front room, also from a transom over the door, and a window that gave some light from the stairs. The children played in the big front room, but they ate, worked, and did their lessons in the kitchen. A single electric bulb dangled there, the only one in the loft. But no light was needed in the front room. After dark a glow from the street lamp poured beneficently through the unblinded windows, and made it fine for undressing, and comforting at night if one awoke hungry and frightened.

The beds were made; the rooms were clean and orderly. Lately Sis had appreciated Mummie with a new and painful knowledge of her difficulties.

Mummie was proud. "This is our home," she told them. "We must keep it as nice as we can."

Mummie rose early and cleaned the loft before she went to work. Mummie came home at night with groceries and cooked them a good supper. Mummie never said she was tired. She was like a brave warrior between them and hunger and cold. Mummie managed. She was thin and "work-brickle";* her red hair was streaked with gray.

Mummie liked their loft. "It's nice here," she told them. "We have it much better than lots of people, and we're never

---

* Worked so hard she had no physical or emotional reserves to fall back on.

41

sick. We're lucky, that's what we are!"

Now Sis plopped George down in his high chair, pulled off his sweater and leggings that had once been hers, while the twins and Edith took off their nondescript wraps and hung them on the low hooks Mummie had screwed inside the kitchen door. Edith set out the dishes on the oilcloth-covered table, and Sis dipped sliced bread in a little milk, and fried it in dripping, and served it with molasses. The children ate it greedily, and Peanut, who had never heard that dogs shouldn't eat bread, licked up his own portion with great gusto, rattling his tin pan all over the kitchen to get the last flavor. All the while they talked.

"And you mustn't tell Mummie, Maggie and Tillie. You mustn't say one word. And George, don't you dast to let it out, or I'll spank you proper!"

The twins glowed with conspiracy.

"Eat," said George, and the girls laughed aloud at this witticism.

George emptied his plate and put it on his head and puffed out his cheeks, and no comedian on earth could ask for an audience more convulsed with mirth. Then, without warning, the little boy laid his cheek on his spoon and went instantly to sleep. Sis put back the tray of his high chair, holding him in place with one hand as she did so. Then she tilted him over her shoulder gently, and took him in and put him in his crib. She wiped the molasses from his hair and face with a wet washcloth and covered him warmly, shoes and all. There he would sleep until Mummie came home a little after five.

The little girls busied themselves with the dishes, then combed one another's hair—with a common comb—and Sis washed faces all around. She put two pieces of coal in the range and shut off the dampers, and they went into the front room to play. Here a pipe from the store below ran up through the room and gave them plenty of heat. The floor was warm, the windows bright with sunshine.

Edith and the twins amused themselves with a penny rubber ball and some old jacks. Then they set up housekeeping with one or two dilapidated dolls. They squabbled, and Maggie cried and beat her heels on the floor, and Mr. Hepstein, the proprietor of the fur store below, rapped on the pipe. Sis spanked Maggie and made her sit on the bed. She was an autocrat. Peanut, with a doll in his mouth, sat up and begged and made Maggie laugh, and the storm was over. The twins, like George, stayed fat and healthy regardless, but Edith was somewhat thin and pale. Sis knew that Mummie worried over Edith, and sheltered her. Sis was thin, too, but with a healthier, stringier quality. She was, perhaps, more like her mother in stamina.

Now the little mother sat down with pencil and paper and confronted the vast problem of thirty-eight cents. It was a tremendous sum, and she had only eight days. Five cents a day she needed. If she could get six! It would be much wiser to count on six cents a day. That would take only seven days, and Sunday Mummie was home. Her mind ranged the neighborhood but found little to encourage it. Mummie absolutely would not let her leave the loft after the early winter dusk had fallen, and all day Sis had to watch the kids. She viewed Edith with a speculative eye. She might leave them now and then when George was sleeping, only Edith could not boss the twins. She cried helplessly when they were naughty.

For a moment Sis was daunted, thinking of their eleven cents. They could have got Mummie something at the dime

store with that. But the vision of the red glass bowl with its gold curlicues came before her eyes and steadied her. They had to do it! She felt the sap rise in her; her nerve grew sure. It was, most likely, the only Christmas present Mummie would have, and she ought to have something really grand, like the red glass bowl, not just a comb from the dime store.

There must be some way she could manage it! There must be! Why, lots of people had ten or fifteen dollars to spend for Christmas, she told herself, although she could not really believe it. She saw that Maggie had tumbled over sideways on the bed, sound asleep. Sis said quietly to Edith and Tilly:

"I'm going downstairs to see Mrs. Hepstein. You two be good, and don't waken Maggie, and you won't have any trouble. And don't let anybody in but me."

She put on her hat and coat, sent the disappointed Peanut back to Edith.

"What are you going down there for, Sis?"

"I want to see if she'll let me work for her until Christmas. I could work a while every day—"

But Mrs. Hepstein was not hospitable to the idea. It was not unkindness.

"You got enough to do, you baby," she said gently. "You can't take on any more chores."

"It's for a Christmas present for Mummie."

"Your Ma wouldn't want you working extra for any present for her," said Mrs. Hepstein. "She doesn't want any Christmas present from you kids, except for you to be good."

"Of course she wants a Christmas present," said Sis indignantly. "Everybody wants one, and Mummie *loves* presents."

"I don't think it's right," said Mrs. Hepstein firmly. "Your Ma pays the rent every month, and she keeps you kids fed and dressed, and that's enough Christmas present for any widow in these hard times. And you go off working and leave them alone, and they'll be throwing water like they did the last time."

Sis looked guiltily at the streak on the stovepipe that went through the ceiling of the store. There was a long ribbon of rust on it. Sis left hastily.

On the street, she paused. She cocked an ear up the stairway. All was quiet above, and she ventured to the corner.

"Hey, Spike," she said to the forty-year-old newsboy who had a stand there. "Let me deliver some papers for you, will you?"

She unfolded the plan to him and told him how beautiful the red glass bowl was—offered to prove it—in Mr. Phibbs's window.

Spike listened cynically. "Kiss your 'leven cents good-bye, Sis," he told her. "You'll never see it again. Old Phibbs done you out of it."

Sis was staunch. "You let me deliver papers for you, and see."

"OK Half a cent a paper—twelve papers, every day at noon. I got some customers would like the noon edition in their stores before lunch every day, now they can't get out at noon account of Christmas trade. I'll give you the papers, and six cents after you deliver 'em. But you've got to be here at eleven-thirty sharp, and no missing!"

Sis rushed home, radiant. Edith was laboriously reading to Tillie, faking out the words she didn't know, and Tillie admired her with innocent eyes. Peanut danced about Sis, and she stooped to scratch his head. Sis's pencil did astonishing things on the paper. She would have to leave out Sunday, when the stores were closed. But the other seven days would give her forty-two cents on the day before Christmas, at noon. And she would get a penny for each of the little ones in change.

There was no way to manage it, save in a body. So the next day, before half past eleven, the five little Andersons and Peanut, all in a terrific fever of excitement, were at the newsstand. Spike, true to his word, gave Sis the twelve noon editions and a list of the stores where she was to leave them. Even ol' fat George was impressed with the gravity of the occasion and actually walked half way.

It was a great expedition. Their errand gave them *entrée*, and they entered the stores in a gang, and stared, entranced, at everything and everybody. It took them an hour to deliver the twelve papers, and Spike gave Sis a nickel and a penny, and they all took it to Mr. Phibbs before they returned home for their lunch. Mr. Phibbs had taken the red glass bowl out of the window and put it on a shelf behind him. There it glowed like a ruby, and Sis felt that Spike had sadly maligned Mr. Phibbs.

The three days left of the week added eighteen cents to their collection. Sis's arithmetic became complicated.

$$\begin{array}{llll} 11¢ & & & \\ +\ 6¢ & 49¢ & 6¢ & 24¢ \\ +\ 6¢ & -\ 29¢ & \times\ 4 & -\ 20¢ \\ +\ 6¢ & =\ 20¢ & =\ 24¢ & =\ 4¢\ \text{O V E R} \\ =\ 29¢ & & & \end{array}$$

ANOTHER four days. On Thursday they would get the bowl, and Christmas was Friday.

Sunday was always a happy day for the five little Andersons.

Mummie was home all day. Her presence transformed the loft. They had many jokes and games, all of them got a good cuddling, things even tasted differently. The Hepsteins were gone. No one cared how much noise they made. They could throw the ball for Peanut to scramble after. He could bark as much as he liked.

All this particular Sunday there was a delightful air of conspiracy among the children. Screams and hands clapped over mouths saved the secret more than once. Sis and Edith were frozen with terror that Mummie would suspect, but she seemed to notice nothing. Once Maggie gave things clear away, but Mummie had the far-away look in her eyes, and when she looked like that she never heard at all, so Sis breathed freely again.

Late in the afternoon a freezing wind began to blow, and the early dusk was hastened

by great clouds of snow that filled the street and danced and whirled about the street lamp. Sis watched it in anguish. Monday morning it was bitter cold. The world was white with a deep, new snow. Mummie left while George and the twins were still sleeping, left Edith and Sis in charge. She was firm in her farewell.

"You must not go out—any of you—no matter what, unless the place burns down!" she added, smiling a little to hide this ancient fear. "One of you sick, even with a cold, would be too much right now. Sis, I put you on your honor—don't leave the house!"

"But, Mummie, maybe I'll have to go out."

"No," said Mummie. "No, you don't. Your shoes aren't fit, and I don't want you lugging the little ones around through the snow and cold, nor leaving them here alone, either. Peanut—mind the family!"

Peanut put his paws up on her dress, his tail beating furiously. He licked her hand. He watched, bright-eyed, as the door closed. There was nothing for Sis to do, nothing at all, but submit. Fiercely Sis encouraged the others, but her own courage was nothing but desperation. Obediently they stayed within-doors.

It was nice when the fire got hot downstairs; nice when the wind turned west instead of north, so that the front windows were no longer frosted. The children cut out papers and made paper dolls. They watched the endless parade of the street; made up long shows in which they were actors and audience turnabout; played house with elegant pretense; turned down all the chairs, and covered them with a blanket for a cave; dressed Peanut in a variety of garments, romped with him, cuddled him, and used him for a pillow. But in spite of Sis's ingenuity the day lagged. Long before it was time for Mummie to come home, their faces were glued to the cold window, watching the corner where she turned into their street.

It was not until Wednesday afternoon that Sis and the children were allowed to venture forth into the streets again. By then the twins were definitely irritable. Edith had cried all morning. Sis was silent, weighed down by the loss of the red glass bowl. And how they had missed their daily excursions into the street, those little Andersons!

They went at once to Mr. Phibbs' store to learn the worst. Again Sis lined them up outside, while she went in alone.

"I've been looking for you every day," said Mr. Phibbs, astonishingly. "I was worried if you was sick or something."

Sis, with the dignity of tragedy, told him what had happened.

Mr. Phibbs listened. He looked at the little face from which the transfiguring light was gone. He sucked his lower lip. Strange things threatened Mr. Phibbs.

"You come back tomorrow, anyhow," he told her—but Sis saw no good to come of that.

In the street again, she and the little ones lingered, a

doleful group. George, at the expression of Sis's face, puckered up to cry.

Mrs. Hepstein came out of the store next door, and spoke to them, and stooped and patted ol' fat George's cheek. Her purse slipped from under her arm, the clasp broke on the walk, and some change rolled out. A quarter wheeled directly toward Sis, by the window, and quicker than that her foot was on it, and she stood staring into the window, her quick, shallow breath making a fog on the glass. Edith helped Mrs. Hepstein gather up the money and put it all into her hand, and Mrs. Hepstein gave Edith a penny,

Still Sis stood, face averted, struggling, convulsed. But she could not do it. Reluctantly, slowly, she lifted her foot under which the quarter burned like a hot coal, and moved a little, still gazing into the store front. If. Mrs. Hepstein didn't see it—if she went on without it—then the revulsion was complete, and Sis stooped and picked up the quarter and held it out in her hand.

"I guess you didn't see this."

It seemed to Sis that Mrs. Hepstein's black eyes plunged into the depths of her soul, but she only said quietly:

"Thank you, Sis. And here's a penny for you, too."

"No—no, thanks—" said Sis, red and shamefaced, and Mrs. Hepstein went on her way down the street.

Sis immediately took Edith's penny away from her and took it in to Mr. Phibbs.

"You come back tomorrow—don't forget," he told her.

* * * * *

That night, after the little ones were asleep, Mummie left Sis and Peanut in charge, with the door safely bolted, and went out. She came back loaded down with burdens. There was something for each of them. A jumping jack and a ball for ol' fat George, small dolls for the twins, a pencil box and tablet for Edith. There was even a tiny, imitation Christmas tree, with some bright balls from the dime store, and popcorn to pop in the skillet and string on red wool. Mummie hid one package, and Sis knew that was for her! Mummie had spent three round, silver dollars in the cheap stores of the neighborhood, and she had a present for each one, and candy and nuts, and an orange and a banana apiece, and meat for a Christmas pot-roast.

Sis was choked with love and sorrow. How lucky they were to have Mummie! That was their luck, nothing else. And they had no Christmas present for her. Oh, if Sis had not been so wild for the red glass bowl! If she had saved their eleven cents, and added the eighteen cents to it, and the penny from Mrs. Hepstein, it would make thirty cents. They might have bought Mummie a big bottle of perfume with that. It was cruel not to have a gift for the one best of all! Sis shivered to think how she had stepped on Mrs. Hepstein's quarter. Mummie would be hurt to know about that. A feverish desire to be a good girl burned in Sis's heart.

She and Mummie hid the things away until Christmas Eve. Then they would hang up the little ones' stockings, they would fix the tree.

At noon the next day Mummie came home and found her tribe gone out. This gave her a chance to turn up the hem of the new dress she had for Sis.

Out on the street the five little Andersons pressed their noses against the window of Mr. Phibbs's Cut-Price Jewelry store. Customers went in and out. And there, in the window,

was the red glass bowl, with a card in it on which was printed the word "Sold." Sis sighed. Edith struggled with tears. The twins were heavy with woe. Ol' fat George said "tired" in vain, and Peanut sat dejectedly. Mr. Phibbs opened the door, and instinctively the five little Andersons drew back.

Mr. Phibbs beckoned to Sis. His face was shining with pleasure. He grinned at them.

"I was looking for you," he said. "Did you come for your bowl?"

Sis faltered, staring at him hypnotized. The others waited to take their cue from her. Mr. Phibbs plucked Sis by the sleeve.

"Come inside, Sis Anderson."

She followed him. The door closed behind her. Mr. Phibbs took the red glass bowl out of the window.

"Everything in the store we marked down, last night," he said slyly. "The bowl is marked down today to twenty-nine cents. Just think of that, for a bowl once priced a dollar. Simulated cut glass, and absolutely pure gold leaf decoration. For such a price! A hard bargain you drive with me, young lady—waiting off until I mark the goods down. It's all ready for you, and you get a penny in change. And would you like it wrapped plain, or for a Christmas present?"

"For a present," said Sis weakly, while slowly, incredulously, the light which had become oddly essential to Mr. Phibbs poured its pure color over her small face.

Mr. Phibbs, as happy as Sis herself, put the bowl in a white box and wrapped it around with white tissue-paper and tied it with red baby ribbon. He handed it over the counter to her politely, and with it a brand-new penny that looked like gold.

He "positively," as he would have said, looked like Santa Claus. His great eyebrows thinned and spread on his bald brow in a double arch. Let each man be measured by his soul's capacity, and it was Christmas in Mr. Phibbs's wintry heart. Sis and the little Andersons had been too much for him.

Dazedly Sis murmured her thanks and walked out of the store spellbound.

* * * * *

No chalice ever was borne more proudly or sacredly through the streets than the red glass bowl. Sis was pigeon-toed and almost cross-eyed with the effort by the time she reached the stairs safely. Ol' fat George walked all the way, and the twins guarded Sis on either side, and Edith and Peanut brought up the rear so that no one might jolt her.

Of course, they could not wait to give it to Mummie. There was no slightest possibility of their waiting until Christmas morning. They gave the present to her just as fast as they could get inside the door of the loft, all crying shrilly,

"Chrismus present—Chrismus present!"

Mummie took it with dramatic astonishment. Her loud outcry and joy were satisfactory to the most greedy heart. Mummie actually cried, and hugged and kissed them all. Mummie couldn't believe it was really for her.

"But it looks so awful expensive," said Mummie. "However could you afford it? And for me! I've always wanted a red glass bowl—all my life I've wanted one!"

She put it in the middle of the kitchen table. She went on and on. Her audience knew no surfeit. They told her about it, singly and in chorus. They stood, six of them, around the table, with Peanut's forepaws and his black nose in their midst, and ol' fat George on tiptoe, one chubby hand on either side of

round eyes that just could see over the table top.

"Did you notice the curlicues, Mummie?"

"It's simular cut glass."

"Mummie—see how the light shines through it."

"Mr. Phibbs marked it down last night," said Sis. "We thought we didn't have enough money, but he marked it down and gave us a penny in change."

"God love him for that!" cried Mummie. "It's the nicest present I ever had in my life—my beautiful red glass bowl!"

Margaret Weymouth Jackson (1895–1974) was born in Eureka Springs, Arkansas. A prolific writer, she wrote more than two hundred short stories for magazines such as *McCall's*, *Ladies' Home Journal*, *Woman's Home Companion*, *Saturday Evening Post*, *American Magazine*, *Country Gentleman*, and *Good Housekeeping*, and half a dozen full-length novels. Her stories celebrate the enduring values found in villages and towns scattered across the American heartland.

The Christmas Year

Rebecca Harding Davis

When the roof of her world caved in and almost crushed her, Ms. Jane, town postmistress, belatedly realized that, in her close-to-death sickness, she had lost Christmas. How on earth might she recover it? This true story reveals how.

* * * * *

From a little Southern village comes to us the story of a woman who once lost Christmas out of her year. Just before the day, misery and disgrace, and, at last, crime came into her family. She carried the load for a while, and then fell under it, sick unto death. The blessed day dawned and passed, but she was lying unconscious and knew nothing of it. When she came to herself the people of the town had forgotten that there ever had been a Christmas. But the day had always counted for much to Jane. It seemed to her like a word of cheer from God Himself on her weary climb upward, giving her hope and strength and encouragement for the whole year to come.

Jane ran the village post-office. She was apt to be sharp and cross, because she was old, and had a secret ailment which at times tortured her. But when she took up her work on the very first day that she was able to do so, it suddenly occurred to her:

"Why not pretend that this is Christmas Day, and keep it, though nobody but God and me will know?"

She opened the window, and as she gave out the letters had a cordial word for every one of the neighbors outside—children and hard-working women and feeble old men. They went away laughing and surprised, but strangely heartened. When the office was closed, she bethought herself of gifts, and baked some of her famous crullers and carried them to folk so poor that they never had any crullers, and to the old paupers in the poorhouse.

She astonished each of them, too, with the gift of a dollar.

I can do with my old cloak another year, she thought, *and they will feel rich for days!*

"In His name," she said to herself as she gave each of her poor presents.

The little gifts held out for a long time as she carried them from house to house, her face growing kinder as she went and her voice softer. It seemed to her that never before had there been so many sick, unhappy folk in the town. Surely it was right to make them glad that He had come among us—even if it were not Christmas Day.

She was very tired when she had finished her day's work. She thanked Him when she knelt down at night that He had put it in her mind to keep His day in this secret fashion.

But she could not sleep for thinking of other poor neighbors to whom she might have given some little comfort or pleasure.

Why not make them happier that He has come, to-morrow, as well as to-day? she thought, with a shock of delight in her discovery.

So it came to pass that this little postmistress made a Christmas out of every day in that year for her poor neighbors. When

The Christmas Year
by Rebecca Harding Davis

she had no more gifts for them, she threw herself into their lives; she nursed them when they were sick, helped them up when they fell, cried with them when they suffered, and laughed with them when they were happy.

And thus it was that she taught them of her Master, and led them to be glad, every day of the year, that He had been born into the world to be its Helper.

Rebecca Harding Davis (1831–1910) was born in Washington, Pennsylvania; later the family settled in Wheeling, West Virginia. Her *Life in the Iron Mills*, initially published in *The Atlantic Monthly* in 1861, is regarded by many critics as a pioneering document marking the beginning of realism in American literature. Among her friends were Emerson, Alcott, and Hawthorne. Recurring themes in her works are the American Civil War, race, regionalism, the working class, and women. Her first son, Richard Harding Davis, became a famous writer and journalist as well.

The Little Brown House

Marie Conway Oemler

The Senator's wife had everything she'd ever dreamed of having. And her husband had achieved everything he set his hand to. They still had each other, but she knew that wasn't true. They'd lost each other somewhere along the way.

Suddenly she began to long for all she'd lost: "Old neighbors, old faiths, old friends, old simplicities. She had advanced—but to what? What, of all the great essentials, had she gained? In all this success, what was hers—to keep?"

Then, her car rolled slowly by "the Little Brown House" with a "For Sale" sign nailed to its front porch . . .

* * * * *

The Senator's wife was returning from the very smartest of afternoon affairs; her white-haired and fresh-colored loveliness had charmed and delighted the most famous and fastidious of diplomats, and the Chinese minister had expressed frank amazement at the magical youthfulness of the American Grandmother; as she stepped into her car the magically youthful rose still blew in her cheeks.

To avoid a crash, her chauffeur had made a detour, swung

down two or three residential streets, slipped through the region of fashionable boarding-houses, and turned into a side street, quiet, tree-shaded, peaceful, as if, like the birds, it were going to bed with the sun. On a corner, with a hedge between it and another small house next door, stood the Little Brown House.

The chauffeur wasn't speeding then, so the Senator's wife had a chance to really see the place. It was quite as if the Little Brown House had seen her first, and called out friendly, as one may to one's own.

She came out of her pleasant self-satisfaction with a start; as usual she had been telling herself that she hadn't failed *him*; that step by step she had kept the pace set by his boundless ambition. An international figure now, the West had hammered him out of her giant forge—one of those wonderful Americans about whom some day in the far future, not the Great American Novel alone, but the greatest epic of the entire race is going to be written. Not the least of his successes was the fact that for forty years he had retained the single love and adoration of his wife; she was proud of him with an almost terrible pride.

There had been times when she had wanted to pause, and catch breath, and rest; but always he had been marching upward, and she had gone with him. Once she had thought that afterward—when, say, the children had grown up and settled—they two might grow peacefully and gently old together, in the evening of their days. But that dream had been foregone; she had but grown old youthfully, wonderfully, with a ripening beauty. Now it was only at times, when, disrobed and massaged, she was at last alone, that she admitted she was—tired.

Her social secretary—and *she* knew her social centers like the palm of her hand—said that the Senator's new house was the one perfect house in all America, and those affairs at which his wife presided the most perfect outside of Vienna. She never knew that, deep down in the other woman's soul weariness, a longing for simpler things stung at times like a nettle.

But when her car rolled slowly by the Little Brown House, something broke in her breast; something became alive and fluttered as with wings. Why, it was just such a little house as she had dreamed of, always, in her secretest dreams! It was a pity, she thought, that a great "For Sale" sign was nailed on the front porch, and that all the windows were closed. Little brown houses should never, never be spoiled by "For Sale" signs, and their windows should always be open.

She was going to dine at the White House that night, in a Paris gown, wearing the pearls that the Senator had lately given her. And—she would come home weary. She wished that for just one night out of these gold-and-glory public nights they two might linger over a small table whose simple meal was lighted by the lamp of home. Oh, just for once to be only a gray-haired man and his gray-haired wife, in life's calm closing day, looking steadfastly out into the fading sky, in whose deepening twilight would presently shine, like a beacon, the evening star! No other light save that, and the bedtime candle; no noise, no glitter; no great orchestra, only the dear every-day music of the tea kettle, and the cricket, and the settling log.

The car swung around a corner; the Little Brown House was left behind. She had left behind so much, she thought. Old neighbors, old faiths, old friends, old simplicities. She had advanced—but to what? What, of all the great essentials, had she gained? In all this success, what was hers—to *keep*?

At dinner she met her youngest daughter, married to a title incidental to a big blond Englishman of unimpeachable morals and a goodly rent-roll. The other daughter, Milly, had married the millions of Kilian van Cuypt. Dick, the only son, had married a practically penniless Virginian, but Dick's wife brought connections. The children had all done well: she was satisfied with things as they were; but at dawn she admitted again that she was tired, too tired to sleep.

The Little Brown House crept into her mind soothingly. In the room shaded by that one great tree the lights would long since have been out. That would be a very simple room; the toilet articles wouldn't be of crystal and of hammered gold, for instance; there would be no inlaid and priceless furniture: it would be just dear, and clean, and cozy; after a quiet day one might pass there a quieter night.

She wondered what it would be like—living in a little brown house. Whimsically she lay awake and furnished it, room by room. At first she failed to note the significance of her omissions, the curious sense of rest and freedom which the mere thought of eliminating a great retinue of servants gave her. Little brown houses haven't room for retinues; one had perhaps a little maid whom one really knew, and in whose affairs one was interested. It occurred to her that she knew just about as much of the lives of *her* servants as she knew about the man in the moon. But in little brown houses one might come into pleasant human contact with one's few necessary helpers. She surmised that this was the right way, the good way, the Galilean Carpenter's way.

The Carpenter!

Her thoughts drifted back to her girlhood's churchgoing, the churchgoing of people in little homes, who have sometimes not enough, sometimes just enough, but never, oh never, too much. Of a sudden she remembered her mother's sweet untrained soprano, her father's stern bass:

Abide with me—fast falls the eventide,
The darkness deepens—Lord, with me abide!

And her mother had had but one best cashmere; her father a sacred suit, religiously laid out on the bed of a Sunday morning!

There had been Wednesday-night prayer-meetings; she had gone, a little, little girl, holding tight to the hired girl's hard, kind hand. She wondered, with a tightening of the heart, what had become of Martha. Perhaps she was some gray-haired grandmother tonight; perhaps Martha too slept under the stars and the night wind and the grass, in a corner of that old cemetery wherein, lying very close together, her own father and mother rested.

How calm and serene those two time-worn faces had been! The simplicity of their lives and their faith seemed to make a deeper gulf between her and them than death or years. As in a dream she remembered the quavering voice of their oldest friend reading over them:

"... *the love of God ... the grace of our Lord Jesus Christ ... the fellowship of the Holy Ghost.* ..."

Ah, but to them these things had been the real and the essential— "the substance of things hoped for, the evidence of things not seen!" To her they had been for many a year but empty echoes, to which one listened, if one listened at all,

with polite inattention and unemotion.

And then she thought with astonishment, *Why, perhaps they succeeded, who held fast to things they were never to lose; perhaps it is we who fail—we who have only the things we can touch with our hands.* In her carved and lace-hung bed, which had cost more than all the furniture in her father's house, she began to weep softly; but as if those tears had cleared her vision she saw what she might do.

The Senator was more than scrupulous about his wife's more than liberal allowance: it was a very easy matter for her to purchase the Little Brown House. *Never, she thought, had the mere possession of any one thing given her so much pure pleasure.*

It wasn't, however, the sort of house you can furnish by a wholesale order at the nearest furniture store. No, indeed; you have to hunt carefully for things to put into little brown houses. Piece by piece the Senator's wife found her belongings: here an old dresser, there an old chair or an older table; all good and solid and beautiful, with the beauty of being *lived with*.

She was tired of the pitiless bright glare of gas and electricity; so on her dining-table stood a softly shaded family lamp. The sort of lamp *you* used to sit around, once, long ago, while your brother and your sister studied their lessons near-by, and your mother, a stocking of yours on her hand, looked up, smiling, from time to time to answer your many questions; and your father twinkled over his glasses and his paper at all of you. You remember now, don't you? You wouldn't take anything life might offer, for just that memory, would you? And isn't it strange that, looking back at them now that they've gone, just these simplest memories seem somehow the holiest?

Upstairs the bedrooms, all in freshest dimity, and smelling of lavender and rosemary, begged you to come in and lie down and rest a while. And you didn't need to look at the Unrevised Version on a stand by the bed to know that they were rooms you could *pray* in. On the wall in the front room hung, in a blackened frame, a sampler, a nice moral sampler, with an edging of painfully prim flowers, "Work'd by Anne Alice Hardy, Age'd 12 yrs." Anne Alice was the Senator's wife's mother; and the sampler had lain for years at the bottom of a trunk, because, among the notable pictures on the walls of the great new house, there wasn't room for anything so crude.

When with loving exactitude the Little Brown House of dreams had been wrought into reality, the Senator's wife drew a long breath of relief. She said with a smile and a sigh:

"Now I need flowers, and a cat, and a canary, and a friend."

Getting flowers, and a cat, and a canary do not present difficulties; getting a friend does. The Senator's wife knew exactly what she wanted; she knew that the Little Brown House must spell happiness, and home, and hope to any who were to dwell therein.

Face after face flitted through her mind, to be dismissed. The social secretary? *She* despised little brown houses! The Senator's wife began to wonder if, perhaps, people do not build great houses more to please social secretaries, and visitors, and butlers, and footmen, and maids than to live and be happy in themselves!

Apply to the pastor of her church? But he too was one for whom the bigger houses are built. Her friends? Fashionable friends are—acquaintances. They would smile to one another, with lifted eyebrows, over their bridge-tables, if they knew.

Her husband? Never, never, never him: he was with all his heart and soul a man of his times; never was he to know that

the high place he had coveted and won for her wasn't her ideal realized.

The Little Brown House remained closed, and dark at night when a friendly light should have streamed through its windows. Every time she walked through its homey rooms—rooms which seemed to be complaining of not being allowed to be home—the Little Brown House asked reproachfully:

"You who have so much, haven't you one, just one, real friend you can share my simple secret with? Why, those you regard as utter failures can call in friend and neighbor to share their joys and sorrows. Do you know why? Because Just-Enough, and more often Not-Enough, draw folks together brotherly; but Too-Much cuts you off from your kind.

"Why do you come, Senator's wife, to me, who am only a little brown house, and keep me empty? You must share me—or leave me!"

Among her charities were several Homes for women—women that haven't any homes of their own, and that nobody on earth wants in theirs. Her name figured on their lists of patronesses and on their many boards. And while the social secretary attended to all the mere business details, and she had but to sign the necessary checks, she made it a rule to appear at each annual function, exquisitely gowned, smiling, affable, a being from another sphere almost.

The price that one insensibly pays for Too-Much is that one insensibly forgets one is just folks; the whole great toiling wonderful terrible race becomes to one—the common people. Just as if all that has been created in our common universe hadn't been made by our common God for His common people!

The Senator's wife, naturally enough, drifted into this common error. It wasn't that she didn't feel kindly—why, she wished to help—with checks. But she simply couldn't imagine that people who had nothing at all could be just like herself. So she had never looked at any one face among all these faces to know it from its fellows: these were just the faces of old women in Homes.

* * * * *

It was only because the Little Brown House was so insistent in its demands, making her thoughtful, that she found herself watching at one of these sad receptions the strong serene face of Anne O'Driscoll. Moved by a sudden impulse, she approached the middle-aged woman, who was looking about her with the merry courage of Irish eyes.

"I hope," she began, "that you're happy here?" Her voice hadn't the usual complacent sureness of the grateful reply.

"My two eyes," said Anne O'Driscoll after a pause, "went back on me last winter, an' I could sew no more. I'm too old to find payin' work, though I'm too young, I'm thinkin', for *this*. But I'm grateful for the shelter, ma'am, for I'd been alone and sick."

"Alone and sick!" The sheltered and beloved woman shuddered slightly. "I'm sorry Mrs.—Mrs.—"

"Thank you kindly, ma'am, but I'm used to it—the being alone—for a good many years. An' I'm no Mrs., but just Anne O'Driscoll."

"You aren't unhappy here, at least?"

"I'd be less so, ma'am, if I'd the hopes of gettin' work, an' my cat Blinkie back. I minded losin' Blinkie most of all, I think. Ah, he was a fine cat, an' more knowin' than most folks, Blinkie was!"

"And you couldn't bring him here? Why, the very idea, wanting and not being able to keep—just a *cat*!"

"Why, ma'am," said Anne gently, "you couldn't expect the Home to take you an' your cat too. Just think now, if we'd all be allowed to bring what we liked with us—this one a cat, and t'other one a dog, and another one a parrot, might be! Oh, no, ma'am, it wasn't to be expected; so I let Blinkie go to the grocer on the corner's wife, that'd always wanted him. If you're to keep things yourself you must have a home that's yours to keep them in." There wasn't the faintest trace of bitterness in her voice.

An old woman, plain, unlettered; an old cat that she couldn't keep: could anything be more *banal*? But Anne looked something like her own old aunt, her father's sister, dead these many years.

"May I," said the Senator's wife, "call you Anne?"

"Why, of course, ma'am, if you like." Anne was neither flustered nor flattered by the great lady's notice, just simply and pleasantly responsive.

"Anne," said the lady after a pause, "Anne, don't you think you'd like a really truly home, where you'd grow old gently and in peace and surety, with enough work to make things worth-while, and not enough money to spoil things, and a cushion in the sun for Blinkie, and flowers in the windows—and—somebody else to help, Anne?" Her voice was a bit breathless.

"There's women," said Anne softly, "that's born to ache for a home all their days, an' never do they find nor keep it. I'm one of 'em."

The Senator's wife wondered a little at herself. She had known Anne but a few minutes; Anne was a plain woman, a woman in a Home, and she knew that she was going to tell Anne all about the Little Brown House; and Anne would understand!

"Will you come with me to-morrow, Anne, to see a little brown house that needs somebody—and I think that somebody's you—to take care of it?"

Over Anne's face fell an autumn fairness of emotion. She lifted humid eyes.

"To-morrow, then!" said the Senator's wife, delicate finger on lip. "And, remember, it's a secret, Anne."

She came for Anne in her big new car, and together they went over the Little Brown House. Anne had fingered the table-cloths and towels and bed-linen lingeringly, and laid her hand on the shining tables with a loving touch.

"You like it, then?" asked the Senator's wife. Anne began to cry for answer. And after the Senator's wife, seated beside her on the chintz-hung sofa, had explained things, Anne took the white hand in her brown one.

"Dear heart! To think you were like that all along, underneath, an' me thinkin' you weren't anything but just a fine lady!" she wondered. "I'm thinkin' it's a grand thing, now, to be a fine lady, because women's women; that's all they be—thank God!" She lifted her head, and the other woman saw, not admiration nor flattery nor envy, but love, real love, look at her out of the eyes of a friend.

As they shut the door of the Little Brown House after them, they heard through the open windows of the house next door the painfully measured splashing of "Silvery Waves" spilled over a piano by childish fingers.

"Why, we've got neighbors!" said the Senator's wife gaily. "I'd forgotten *that*. And we're neighbors too, aren't we? Anne, after a while you must send things over on a tray, and we hope

they'll be neighborly and just drop in when they can. Isn't it nice, Anne? And after they've called on you, you must tell me all about them. I hope they've got *little* children. We'll give their little girl a doll, and their boy a train of cars, won't we? My little grandson dotes so on trains of cars!"

* * * * *

When she could come, between whiles, she found herself in the midst of a pleasant neighborhood life; and all about her were the soft noises and sights and smells of home. Anne's pride in the place was almost piteous. How clean and sweet it was; how everything was polished, and how it shone and twinkled; but nothing was fussy and not-to-be-used! The neighbors whom she began to meet knew and accepted her as the Lady Who Came to See Anne. They didn't wonder she liked to come to see Anne: they liked to come too.

Next door was a mother of six. They had all come over to see Anne, and Blinkie had purred over the baby. Anne had given all of them little cakes that bound them to her forever. She was going to have the whole noisy, hungry, beautiful brood of them once a week to tea. Anne reveled in their company.

"You know," she told the Senator's wife, "I'd never much of a home at best, Miss Barbara, me bein' out all day, workin'. So I'd no chance of knowin' little children, except I'd see them on the street, an' have to take out my love o' them in passin'. Why, I've known me to be happy for a whole long day because a little thing in its carriage waved its hand an' gave me a smile, passin' by. Now, thanks be to God an' you, I've got a real home, an' a chance to have them about me a bit, though they're none o' my own. I look forward all week to the time they'll come, an' the noise they'll make, an' the joy o' them, an' the way they'll look, an' talk, an' laugh. Miss Barbara, I'm thinkin' this is the kind of a house that *likes* to have children under its roof; an' there'll be more an' more o' them comin' by an' by. An'—you wouldn't be mindin' if I called in, one or two at a time, the old women that's got to stay on in the Home, Miss Barbara? They're tired, sometimes, of just havin' to keep alive, an' a day here'd hearten them, maybe. I'd like to share."

The Senator's wife looked about her. It *was* the sort of house that likes to shelter the young and call in the old and the poor for warmth and kindliness.

"Have them all, Anne. And tell me all about it afterward. You dear, dear woman, you!"

"I'd most forgotten to tell you about the Westerner, hadn't I? The lady next door brought him first, Miss Barbara, him bein' a great friend o' the children's. An' he's the clearest-eyed, softest-spoken, brownest-faced man ever I clapped my two eyes on. Right around the corner from us he is, him keepin' house by himself, except for the passel o' men that's always comin' to set with him. I ain't one for praisin' up men-folks' housekeepin', Miss Barbara; so one day I upped an' sent him a tray—a big heavy one at that, jest to show him! He brought it back himself, him havin' no servant, an' he was that kind an' sociable I took to him like the children do. I like Westerners—they're so just *themselves*, ain't they? He's real glad we're neighbors, he says, an' him an' his friends'll be glad to be of any service to us. I told him us bein' women-folks an' the best cooks, they'd better come over an' neighbor with us holidays. The nicest man ever I knew, Miss Barbara—it's him fixed our kitchen-window shelves."

The Senator's wife smiled appreciatively, then went

upstairs for her usual half-hour of quiet thought and rest by that shaded window. Outside the day was rather dark, and the tree was bare now to the autumn winds. She sat with her hands in her lap thoughtfully. The Senator hadn't been so well of late. He looked, she thought, more gray and old.

Why, it's getting so we just see each other going up and down stairs! she thought indignantly and sorrowfully. *We're getting old too, Hugh and I are. Oh, it isn't fair, it isn't fair! We aren't even sharing any more—I can't share his work, and he won't share my house!*

* * * * *

That was perhaps the most strenuous winter either of them had known. They crossed each other's orbits frenziedly. At her affairs he showed his fine work face for a few dutiful minutes, then disappeared. And when at times they did go out together, the usual tactful hostess, following immemorial custom, separated them.

In the midst of this mad swirl Christmas drew near. To the Senator's wife Christmas had come to mean merely a long list of gifts, dutifully checked over with her secretary: you gave just as you received; you had to. You knew that from the housekeeper down every one in the house must be remembered; the secretary saw to it that they were. There was no planning; no hiding of things half done when somebody came into the room; no mysterious hints nor smiles; no air of subdued eagerness; no tender sacrifices that make gifts doubly precious.

But at the Little Brown House things were different. Anne had made with her own skillful hands something for everybody: for the little Maid Who Helped; for the Mother of Six and her brood; for the old women from the Home; for the Man Around the Corner, who was so glad to be neighborly; and for the Senator's wife. Anne even had a tree; and they were all to come for a while on Christmas Eve, except, perhaps, Miss Barbara.

"I wish," said Anne, looking up from the cake she was whisking together, "that you'd put on your plainest frock, Miss Barbara, and come. It'd make Christmas more like Christmas as it ought to be, for me." Her eyes implored the Senator's wife with so much of love and longing that the heart in her warmed anew to Anne.

"The Senator and I have simply got to attend our daughter's Christmas Eve reception, but I think, by close management, I *might* manage to get here—from half-past six until nearly nine, say. And I could drive home and dress, and nobody'd be the wiser for my pleasantest Christmas secret!" She thought for a moment, and laughed like a girl: "Anne, I'm coming!"

The Senator was to accompany her to their daughter's. She knew that until then she wouldn't see him; she knew, too, that some beautiful and costly gift, chosen with exquisite care, would be lying by her plate on Christmas morning. No, he wasn't forgetful, nor neglectful, any more than she herself; he was only—too busy.

* * * * *

It was quite half-past seven when she reached the Little Brown House on Christmas Eve. When she opened the door she knew that Christmas itself had arrived before her; for the house was alive with young children, as all self-respecting

houses would be if they had the chance. You heard the children's shouts, and their mothers' worried admonitions, and Anne's cheerful, "There, there, let 'em be! It's Christmas Eve, an' Christmas Eve's children's eve. Ay, my dearies, laugh, do! An' when Miss Barbara comes we'll open that settin'-room door; an' then you'll see what you'll see—bless you!"

"Miss Barbara" came in to be swallowed in a warm sea of joyous welcomings. She wore what she considered a plain dress; but the Mother of Six, and the women with her, looked upon its lustrous folds almost with awe; only the Baby disregarded it, and sat upon it, and kicked his feet against it unconcernedly.

The sitting-room door had been opened; they were in the midst of gift-giving, and receiving, and exclamations when the door-bell rang.

"That," said Anne, pausing, with the Baby's jumping-jack in her hand, "Will be that Westerner from 'round the corner. I'll let him in, Miss Barbara; he'll want to stay with the children here for a while, I know."

The Senator's wife heard the front door open and close, and men's feet in the hall, and the Westerner saying in his pleasant out-of-doors voice full of the burr of R's:

"Here's a bunch of real holly, and some real mistletoe to hang up; and here's my oldest friend along with me—he's an old friend of those kids' too. We've brought you a few things to add to the tree for 'em. Say now, it sure makes us two old chaps feel right good and Christmassy to get in here with you women and kids tonight."

Anne and the Westerner came in together. The other man followed more slowly, looking about him with merry eyes. He was a very, very big man, and he seemed to fill in the whole doorway in which he stood. Then the children saw him, and shouted rapturous welcomings; and he returned these with somewhat of a tender wistfulness in his smile.

From her sofa the Senator's wife looked up; their eyes met, incredulously. She rose to her feet, putting down the Baby.

But Anne had advanced to him, holding out a friendly hand.

"I know you're the Big Man That Plays with the Children!" she said cordially. "I'm sure glad to meet you at last, Neighbor; welcome, an' a Merry, Merry Christmas to you!"

He returned her greeting cordially; then the Senator's wife came forward. Her eyes were large.

"You!" she said faintly. "You—neighbor—playing with children. You here!"

"You!" said the Senator. "Here, tonight—why, Barbara, my dear!"

"I come—when I can find time—Anne keeps house—" she began.

He nodded. "I go around to Jack's—when I can find time. One's got to have a few friends one can visit, don't you think?"

The Baby set up a great wail, because he was a baby, and he had had enough of presents, and play, and grown-ups; and he wanted to go home and be put to bed. The Mother of Six picked him up, and her friends gathered the rest of the brood and their belongings together and carried them off, with many Christmas wishes tossed back and forth.

Anne beckoned the Westerner into the dining-room and pointed to the table.

"No real gentlemen," said she, "will refuse to fall to an' help eat up a lady's pie that she's made with her own hands for Christmas."

"I am," said the Westerner, "a long-fanged wolf on pie. An' if you'll cut yours in just halves, I'll be everlasting grateful to you, ma'am." And he sat down, turning his back upon the sitting-room door.

The Senator and his wife came to each other slowly, he looking down upon her whimsically, she looking up at him with eyes of pure wonder.

"Why, Barbie, is there ever any reading a woman? I'd never guess that you'd come visiting a little house like this—"

"This little house," she said, "is mine: I bought it. I've wanted just this little house all my life, and I wasn't honest or brave enough to tell you so."

"I thought," said the Senator, "that it was the other sort of house you wanted, Barbie. That's why I built it—for you."

"I did want it and I do want it—for you," said his wife. "That's why I let you build it. But I want this for *me*—to get rested in, to be folksy in."

A slow twinkle grew in the Senator's eyes.

"Barbara," he said, "you ought to see Jack's house, around the corner! A mighty nice little house. I've been going there for a long time. Didn't you ever guess I might like to be just folksy too, Barbie? There's no tiresome bunch of servants tagging at your heels at Jack's. You can sit down in your shirt-sleeves and smoke a cuddy, if you want to; you can wait on yourself without shame and reproach—think of that! Do you know what Jack had for supper to-night? Fish-chowder, and pan-bread, and coffee that'd make your hair curl! It was good!

"You see," he went on thoughtfully, nodding his head, "I like to go to Jack's because I get rested there—he's a man. I can quarrel with him, even! Now you know I've loved you, and you alone, all my life, Barbie; it's for you I wanted—the top-notch. But I—get tired at times. I want to loaf a little, and be folksy too. And you, Barbie, you?"

"I also," said the Senator's wife with a girl's laugh. She put her arms about his neck and clung to him. "Oh, Hugh, my dear, don't you see, we've come together again! Hugh, we've come together, close! It wasn't the big house, nor the too muchness: it was that we didn't know, Hugh, and we couldn't take time to find out! All these years—and I didn't know the real You until to-night; all these years, and you had to stumble by chance into the Little Brown House on Christmas Eve, and find the real Me."

He kissed her with a young delight that shook his years from him, and straightened his shoulders, and kindled his face; so, for a while, they held each other.

"I wonder," he said presently, "Barbie, I wonder if you or any other woman can keep a secret?"

She waved her hand about the room by way of reply.

"Why, of course you can, all of you!" said the Senator. "There's no end to the wonder of women! Well, now, Barbie, here's the secret: I'm to take a two weeks' rest after New Year's, and dodge everybody. I'd thought of running out West—but, say, let's just come right here to this little house of yours, and get acquainted all over again, Barbie. I feel as if I didn't half know you anyhow. Will you come, dearest dear?"

"I'll come," she said with shining eyes. "Hugh, Hugh, I'm beginning to fall in love with you all over again—and I fifty-seven and a grandmother!"

The Senator took out his watch. "There's the girl's reception, Barbie—we've got to fly," he said regretfully. "Is the car to come for you?"

"Oh, let's tell Anne to send it back, and we'll walk home,—like we used to—remember?—when a callow fledgling of a country lawyer courted and married a penniless district schoolteacher?"

He nodded, wrapping her carefully in her sables. Anne and the Westerner asked no questions, expressed no surprise, made no comments: they were just such friends as that! They shook hands with a warm and loving pressure, and wished a million Merry Christmases with all their heart. And the Little Brown House breathed after them a message of peace and of understanding; and overhead the sky was thick with stars—one, larger and brighter than the others, dominating a great clear space.

They walked along together, hand in hand. The great holiday crowd jostled them, and they, being afoot, knew themselves a part of it and caught its spirit, and were glad. After a while the Senator glanced up and called her attention to the biggest star.

"The same old Star!" said he softly.

"And we together under it!" she answered happily.

"Why, come to think of it, so is everybody else!" said the Senator with a hint of reverence.

"So is everybody else!" she repeated. "And that," she added, "is just what makes Christmas *Christmas*!"

Marie Conway Oemler (1879–1932) was born in Savannah, Georgia. Mostly homeschooled, she didn't begin writing for publication until she was in her late thirties. She then wrote a series of novels, including *Slippy McGee*, which was made into two movies. She was a regular contributor to *Woman's Home Companion* and other popular magazines.

Home for Christmas

Maude W. Plummer

Christmas wouldn't be Christmas without going home. It was very clear to Deana—not at all clear to Ted.
And little Susie was caught in the middle.

* * * * *

Deana stood at the window watching the big feathery snowflakes that were fast turning the drab little midwestern town into a Yuletide picture.

As the twilight deepened, one by one the windows up and down the street lighted up as someone turned on the colored tree lights. Christmas! In a strange new way it was pressing in on her on every side.

Ted had hung wreaths in all the windows, and now he was fastening mistletoe to the colonial lamp that hung in the middle of the room.

"Come here, darling," he called. "I need your help."

"What is it?" she asked.

"Just this," he said as he caught her close in his arms and kissed her lips. "You're under the mistletoe, you know."

"Me too, Daddy! Me too," little Susie cried as she tugged at their knees.

Ted caught her up and tossed her high, until her golden curls touched the mistletoe. Then he kissed her hair and her cheeks while she squealed in delight.

"Daddy's own two sweethearts," he said, and for a moment he held them both close against himself.

"Shall we have a fire in the fireplace?" Deanna asked as she gently withdrew from his arms. He wasn't making it easy for her to tell him of her decision.

Ted touched the match to the kindling and the flames leaped up spreading a soft glow over the room. He leaned back against the mantel and looked about him.

"Isn't it nice, darling?" he said. "And doesn't it look like Christmas even before we get the tree?"

Yes it was nice, this room—this home she and Ted had built together. The few pieces of fine old maple, the braided rugs, bright slip covers and gingham curtains gave the room a feeling of warmth and security. They had chosen Early American because Ted said it stood for strength and things that endured.

Deana looked at Ted as the firelight played on his dark face—so kind and yet so strong. She should be the happiest girl in the world, and yet—

"Why so quiet and serious, darling?" he asked as his eyes met hers.

"Ted," she said as she crossed to his side. "I'm going home for Christmas."

"But Deana, we've been all through that. You know it's impossible for me to get away at this time of year—inventory and everything."

"Then Susan and I shall go alone," she said firmly.

"But darling, we've made our plans for Christmas here," Ted said. "I've already ordered the turkey. And I was having the tree sent up tomorrow. We'll have great fun trimming it—just you see."

Then he put his arms around her and drew her gently to the davenport. "Let's sit down and get this all straightened out again."

"There's nothing to straighten," she said. "I just can't bear to leave them there alone."

"But they're not alone. They have each other just as we do," he said gently.

"We have Susie. That's what made me decide—Susie. If I had to be away from her, I just couldn't bear it. That's all."

"But darling, when you were Susie's age they did have you. And when Susie grows up—"

"Don't say it, Ted! Don't say it!" she interrupted sharply.

"You must try to understand, you're a mother now as well as a daughter." His voice was kind.

"But I've never missed a Christmas at home, Ted. Even since we've been married, we've always spent Christmas at home. And I can't remember when I

didn't have my party the week before."

"We could have a party here and invite our new friends," Ted offered.

"Oh, Ted, you just won't understand. It isn't just the party. I'm not just thinking of myself. It's Mama and Dad. There'll be nothing for them to look forward to but loneliness."

For a moment he didn't answer. Then in a tight voice, he asked, "And don't you think I'll be lonely if you and Susie are away?"

"Of course, Ted," she said quickly. "But that's different. We're young. There'll be years and years of being together for us. But Mama and Dad aren't so young, and it's harder for them. I just can't be happy here at Christmas when I know I'll be hurting them so much."

"Your line of reasoning is a little twisted, don't you think?" He arose quickly, walked across the floor and then back again. "But if that's the way you feel, go by all means. Spend every Christmas with Mama and Daddy until you grow up. Then perhaps, you can see your own home and family."

"Oh, Ted, I knew you'd see it my way," she cried, ignoring his hurt and bitterness.

"I won't let them know we're coming," she mused as she began to plan for the trip. "We'll just walk in and surprise them. Ted, please phone and see if you can get plane tickets for the east-bound plane. It takes off about twelve tomorrow."

"You may not be able to get reservations at this late date," Ted said.

"There always are last minute cancellations," Deana answered. "And if there aren't, we'll just have to charter a small plane—now that I've made up my mind to go."

There had been last minute cancellations, and Ted got the tickets. Deana was like a child on Christmas morning, all sparkle and excitement.

"Just think," she sang out as she flew about selecting from the wardrobe things she would need to pack. "This time tomorrow night we'll be there. I wonder if they'll have the tree up."

"I wouldn't know," said Ted absentmindedly.

She held up two evening gowns at arms length, one a filmy white, the other a green taffeta. "Which one do you like best, Ted?" she asked. "I can take only one."

"It doesn't matter to me," Ted answered. "But since you ask, the green looks well with your auburn hair. It matches your eyes—Christmas colors, you know."

She spun about on her toes and kissed him on the chin.

"You darling," she said.

* * * * *

Deana looked at her wristwatch. In half an hour they would be landing at the home airport. Susan was fast asleep and Deana leaned back and closed her eyes. She wondered what her mother and father would be doing now. Would they try to carry on as in other years while their hearts were breaking with loneliness? Always before, about this time of year, the big old house was bright with colored lights. There would be houseguests all over the place for all of her friends; even those who lived in distant cities came for her party. It was really a gala affair and something to look forward to from year to year. She supposed it had been lots of work for Mama and Dad. Their greatest happiness had been doing things for her.

After she had married Ted, and even after Susan was born, things hadn't changed much. Until this year they had lived just down the block a few houses and except that she had Ted and Susan extra, her life was much the same.

On Christmas Eve they had always gone over to the big house and stayed all night. The tree, the dinner, and everything were just the same as when she had been a little girl.

That first year after their marriage, Ted had put up a small tree in their own home and had wanted to put their gifts on it, but she had insisted on taking them to Mama's as usual. He had been a little provoked at her, but it didn't last. Then after Susan was born, he had again wanted Christmas at home, but she had made him see how foolish that was when having them would give Mama and Dad so much pleasure.

But this year! She remembered Ted's face as he kissed her good-bye and a pain shot through her heart. He had looked so lonely as he stood there, his shoulders drooping a little, waving to them as the plane took off. How would he spend Christmas? She thought of the brightly decorated house. Perhaps he would invite some of his friends in. But of course not. Everyone would be spending the holiday with their own families and in their own homes. But surely he could have come too if he'd wanted.

She pushed Ted's hurt look out of her mind and pictured

the joy that would be her parents' when she and Susie arrived. She hoped it would not be too much of a surprise for them. After all, they were both getting on a bit.

Soon the stewardess was helping them fasten their safety belts for the landing, and a few minutes later she was in a cab riding down familiar streets on the way to her old home.

As they made the last turn, she closed her eyes, afraid to look. Would it be dark and lonely or would there be a brave attempt to carry on?

"Here we are, ma'am," the driver said as he brought the cab to a stop. "And from the looks of things, they must be expecting you."

Deana opened her eyes quickly. The house was ablaze with lights. A Christmas tree gleamed from the big front window. Cars were parked in the drive and in the side street. She hadn't expected this. What could it mean?

But of course, she thought, *Ted had phoned to her parents and they were welcoming her with the Christmas party.* She paid the driver and, taking Susan by the hand, ran up the steps.

When she opened the door and stepped inside, the happy greeting froze on her lips. These were not her friends, they were friends of her parents. There was happy laughter and music. A buffet lunch was being served in the dining room and in the big parlor a square dance was in progress.

She did not see her mother at once. Then one of the guests looked up and cried out, "It's Deana!" The next moment she was in her mother's arms while Susie was bounding to her grandfather.

"Deana baby. Where did you come from?" Mama asked in surprise. "Where's Ted?"

"We came for Christmas, just Susan and I," Deana said.

"Ted didn't come?" asked her dad after he had set Susie on her feet and kissed Deana.

"No, he couldn't get away," Deana said and wondered why it was so hard to tell them that Ted had not come.

"Well, I expect you want to freshen up and rest a bit after your trip. You know the way to your old room," Mama laughed. "Then if you care to, come down and join the party. Now I must get back to my guests." She was gone, leaving Deana and Susan to go to their room alone.

When she had bathed Susie and tucked her in, Deana threw herself across the bed and stared at the ceiling. The faint sound of laughter and music drifted up the stairs. Her mind kept going in circles. Ted had not phoned. They were not lonely. Even when they had thought her hundreds of miles away, they were not lonely.

They had been glad to see her, she was sure of that. But for the first time in her life, she felt strange in her room, as if she did not belong in it. This room with its frilly white curtains belonged to a girl of long ago. She felt a twinge of loneliness for another room with Ted's things in it, and his dark head on the pillow beside hers. She wondered if he was missing her. She hoped so. She didn't want him to find it too easy to get along without her. Tears filled her eyes. She undressed, got into bed and turned out the light. She did not want to see or talk to anyone tonight.

* * * * *

It was late when Deana awoke the next morning. As she looked at the familiar objects in the room, the last five years were blotted out and she was just a schoolgirl, waiting for her mother to call. Then from the little bed across

the room she heard Susan's voice.

"Mommie, Susie hungry."

"Of course, baby," she answered as she arose quickly, lifted the little girl out of the bed and carried her to the bathroom. She held her close, and the soft warm body against her own felt comforting.

"Where is Daddy?" the little one asked.

"Daddy isn't here. Susie, hold still and Mommie will soon have you ready to go downstairs for breakfast," Deana answered as she quickly bathed and dressed her.

"Daddy get Kismas tree?" Susie asked.

"No, Daddy won't be here for Christmas. Grandpa'll get the Christmas tree."

"Susie want Daddy. Daddy get tree." Tears filled her eyes and she began to cry.

"Don't cry, baby. Hold Mommie's hand tight and down to breakfast we go." Deana felt a pang of guilt. To have her own Dad, she had deprived Susie of hers. Oh, well, she was still a baby, too young to remember, and next year she'd see to it that Ted came with them.

They went down the stairs and into the kitchen. Breakfast for Mama and Dad had been over hours ago, and signs of last night's party had been cleared away. Mama was at the kitchen desk busy with pencil and paper. She quickly put them into the drawer when Deana and Susie entered.

"Oh, good morning," her mother said as she gave each of them a warm kiss. "Just sit down at the table and have your orange juice. I'll have your bacon and eggs in a jiffy."

Deana watched her mother bustling about getting the breakfast ready. *Maybe it would be the same after all*, she thought.

"It's nice to have you home," her mother said. "But I do wish Ted could have been with you."

"Where's Dad?" Deana asked. She did not want to talk about Ted now.

"He had some shopping to do in town—now that you and Susie will be with us."

"You mean you hadn't planned anything?" Deana asked in astonishment although she told herself it was what she could have expected all along.

"Of course, we had plans. But they would hardly be suitable for you and for Susie. We must make new ones, now."

"Can we have things just like always, Mama?" Deana's voice was wistful and very young.

"The tree and dinner can be almost the same, I think. But of course it's too late for your party. Everyone has made other plans by this time."

"Oh, dear, I had so counted on the party," Deana said.

"We had no idea you'd be here," her mother protested. "Anyway, giving our own party last night was about as much as I could have managed."

"But Mama," Deana asked after a short silence. "You did bake the fruitcake and Christmas cookies, didn't you?"

"No, Deana, I didn't. Your father is buying a cake in town this morning."

"Mama!" Deana exclaimed in shocked surprise. "It's Christmas. How could you not do the things that have meant Christmas to us all through the years?"

"Dear, I know it's Christmas. I told you we had plans. They just didn't include fruitcake, cookies, and Deana and Susie."

"Don't tell me your plans didn't include turkey, either."

"No, they didn't. But your father is ordering that, too."

"I just can't understand you, Mama. Every year we've had

things just the same. I couldn't bear to stay away because those were the things that made Christmas for me. I wanted Susan to have them, too." She broke off and tears ran down her cheeks.

"Oh, Mama, I wanted things to stay the same, always," she sobbed.

For a few moments her mother did not speak. Then she said slowly and a bit sternly, "Deana, it's time you grew up. Susie's the baby, not you." Deana looked resentful, and her mother faced her frankly. "Do you love Ted?"

"Of course. You know I do."

"Then you should be with him at Christmas time."

"But, Mama, he wouldn't come. I thought you and Dad would be so terribly lonely," Deana said.

"I have always worked hard to make your home life good—something you would love and remember," her mother explained. "I tried to make each Christmas the same, to build traditions. I wanted you to carry them into your own home along with new ones that you and Ted would build together.

"Don't you see, dear, it's time for me to bow out. It's your time to take the spotlight and build traditions for Susie—things that she will love and remember."

"But what about you, Mama?" Deana's voice trembled. "That leaves you and Dad so alone."

"Your Dad and I plan to entertain our own friends more often. That's why we had the party last night. On Christmas Day we had planned to go to church and then eat out and later watch television or go to a movie. Your happiness is now in Ted's hands, and we can give more time to each other. No matter how much you love them, children are only a part of your life. They go on to homes of their own. It's the husband that's with you always."

Deana arose and went slowly into the living room. She wanted to be alone—to try to think things out. She stared blindly out the window. She had been so sure that without her there would be no happiness for her parents. And it had been nice to feel so needed. Now she felt lonely and unwanted. Ted had been right all the time. Mama and Dad had each other. They would never be lonely. Their love and what they had built through the years was an armor against that. Suddenly she wanted her own husband, very much. Dear Ted. Did he feel lonely and not needed, too?

She thought how patient and kind he had always been, even when she must have been very disappointing to him.

"Oh, Dear God, don't let it be too late! Don't let it be too late," she whispered as she stumbled to the telephone and put in a long-distance call for Ted.

At last she heard his dear voice coming over the wire.

"Deana, darling, is anything wrong?" he asked, his voice full of concern.

"No, Ted. There's nothing wrong. Everything is right. Get the tree and turkey ready. Susie and I will be home on the next plane. We'll have Christmas in our own home—together."

As she cradled the receiver and turned, Susie toddled in.

"Listen, baby," Deana said as she hugged her close. "We're going home to Daddy."

"Daddy get tree," the little girl cried, clapping her hands.

"Yes, dear, Daddy'll get the tree."

And now Deana knew, when she saw the happiness that shone in Susie's eyes, she was doing the right thing.

Maude W. Plummer wrote for popular magazines during mid twentieth century.

Christmas Tonight

Val Teal

It was a week before Christmas, and excitement ran high in the little village house. Such exciting shopping only a day off.

Suddenly, a horse plodded into their lane with its rider slumped over the horse's neck.

After that, not one of their Christmas plans materialized—except, perhaps, Grandmother's.

* * * * *

A *story especially for children.*

* * * * *

Everywhere, everywhere, Christmas tonight," Grandmother was singing softly when Janey came to her door.

"What does that mean?" Janey asked.

"Just that," said Grandmother. "Christmas is everywhere. You can't stop it. You can shut yourself up in a room and lock the door, but Christmas will come in. Christmas is everywhere." She took down a little tin star from her shelf. "I keep this to remind me of that," she said, "and of the best Christmas I ever had, too."

Janey crawled into a corner of the couch. There was the story look in Grandmother's eye.

* * * * *

"I was ten years old that year," Grandmother began. "It was a week before Christmas and the weather was still fine, sunshiny and warm for December. We had a lot of things yet to do for Christmas. I had hardly any of my presents ready. We didn't have all our cookies made yet—although there were perhaps five hundred stored away in the cans. We usually made twice that many so as to have something to 'treat' when the people from the village came to call during the holidays.

"And Mother said she had hardly anything done. We were to go into town the next day. Then we would go to the brightly decorated village shops and complete our shopping. Nicholas, my younger brother, was a Christmas child. He had been born on Christmas and he was named for St. Nicholas, and so Christmas was his special day. This year he wanted only one thing for Christmas and that was a pet—a live pet. Tomorrow we were going to go to see Mr. Abrams and see about getting a puppy for him.

"We were working hard to get everything done so that we might have the day to spend in the town, when a horse turned into our lane. The rider was slumped over the neck of the horse, and we ran out yelling for Father to come.

"It was Sam, the man who lived at our cabin up on the mountain. He had broken his leg and had managed somehow to get onto his horse and ride the twenty miles to town. Father took him into the village and had him looked after. But up on the mountain were the animals to care for. There were Dandy and Dolly, the sheep, and Nanny, the goat. Someone had to go up and get them.

" 'It will make a nice outing for all of us since the weather

is so fine,' Mother said. And so we packed up a huge basket of food, and the next morning very early we all piled into the lumber wagon. Dandy and Dolly and Nanny would come back in the wagon with us.

* * * * *

"Twenty miles, most of it uphill, is a long trip for two horses. It was afternoon when we arrived at the cabin. Father went around and made everything tight against the coming winter weather. We would stay overnight and in the morning lock up the cabin and take the animals home with us. Nicky and I went to bed early. We tried to stay awake and call back and forth to each other from our bunks, but the long day out-of-doors and the dancing light of the fire made us so sleepy we were soon in slumberland.

"When I awoke, it seemed to be the middle of the night. Father was talking excitedly. He had a lantern lit. There was another noise too. The fire was roaring, but it was still another noise, above that. I sat up in bed and listened. It was the wind, howling round the cabin. Mother told me there was a blizzard and that I had better go back to sleep for a few hours. It felt good to snuggle down under the blankets again and when Nicky and I woke the next time, it was dimly daylight. Mother was making pancakes and we could smell coffee.

"We ran to the window, but we could not see out. The snow was piled way up to the top. Father had shoveled his way out to the shed to care for the animals, and he had tied a rope to the door knob and taken it with him so that he could find his way back.

"All day the blizzard howled. The snow would blow down the chimney and make the fire dance and sizzle. We were in a world alone. Beyond the cabin there was nothing but blowing snow and howling wind. I went to the shed with Father once, and the top of the snow was above my shoulders. At any other time Nicky and I would have thought this was great fun, but now all we could think of was Christmas. Father said there wasn't a chance that we could get home for many days.

"When Nicky went out to the shed with Father, I threw myself on my bunk and sobbed. Mother came in and patted my shoulder.

" 'It will still be Christmas,' she said. 'You can't stop Christmas with just a blizzard. It comes wherever you are. It will be wonderful—you wait and see.'

" 'But the presents,' I cried. 'And Nicky won't get his puppy!'

" 'When Christmas comes,' Mother said, 'presents come. We'll find presents. Come on. Let's look around.'

* * * * *

"There were five more days until Christmas, and a busier bunch of people there never was than we four up there by ourselves on the mountaintop. Father had said he would dig around in the snow and find a tree and chop it down. So the next thing Nicky and I thought of was paper chains to trim it with. But an old bachelor like Sam didn't have colored paper and paste around his house. Sam did save things, though. We found lots of colored comics. We made flour and water paste. And Nicky and I spent the entire day making paper chains.

"The next day the snow had stopped. Father shoveled it away from the windows, but all we could see as far as we could

look was snow. About noon he brought in our tree—a lovely middle-sized one. We hung our paper garlands on it.

"Then Father had an idea. We got out a basket of empty tin cans from the back shed, and Father cut dozens of these little stars. Nicky and I pounded a hole in one point of each star with a nail so that we could put string through them and hang them on the tree. The tree looked wonderful.

"Mother was busy making cookies. There were flour and sugar, and cream from the goat's milk. Sam didn't have any cookie cutters, but Mother used a can and Father bent a piece of tin into a shape of a Christmas tree and we cut out men with a knife. I put one of the stars on the rolled-out dough and cut around it with a knife and we had star cookies, too. Mother baked string loops into some, and we frosted them and hung them on the tree.

"Presents. I kept thinking and thinking. I found a pile of carefully folded wrapping paper. Mother helped me iron out the largest pieces. I cut them even and sewed them into a grand large scrapbook for Nicky. I looked through the magazines and started the book for him with a picture of some horses and another of a dog. Maybe he wouldn't mind too much not getting his live pet.

"This was the idea we got for presents for Mother and Father: We took two little tin pie tins from Sam's cupboard. We filled them with scraps from some old worn-out overalls of Sam's and covered them with two good pieces of the blue denim. Now we had two puffy pin cushions. We cross-stitched Mother on one and Father on the other.

"Christmas morning came, and there were several packages under the tree. Mother and Father were very pleased with our pin cushions. Father said it would always remind him of his favorite food, pie, and then when he opened Mother's gift, it was a real pie. Mother had managed to make it out of canned cherries. Nicky and I each got new mittens from Mother. Mine were blue with a white duck knitted on to the backs, and Nicky's were red with white men. Nicky had made me a penwiper, and he had cut out a paper doll family for me from a catalog. Out of kindling wood and spools Father had made a darling little wheelbarrow for Nicky and a whole set of doll furniture for me. The paper doll family just fit the furniture. It seemed the very nicest Christmas I had ever had. The blazing fire was reflected in every one of our tin stars. There was a good smell of spicy cookies and other cooking Mother had been doing.

"Suddenly, Mother got up and went out into the back shed. She came in with a shoe box with holes punched in it. Inside was a chipmunk, and I think I was as happy over it as Nicky.

"'He got caught in the shed when the blizzard came,' Mother said.

"It was wonderful. Everything was turning out right. But there was work to be done.

"I opened the door to sweep the snow from the stoop. I heard a little scuttle at the side of the stoop. I still can hardly believe that I found just what I wanted, but there indeed was a live pet for me to give Nicky. A white rabbit had burrowed into a hollowed-out place in the snow drift beside the step. He let me pick him up by the ears, and I ran into the house shouting, 'Merry, *Merry* Christmas, Nicky!'

"And right then Father came to the door from the shed and said, 'Come on out, children, I have another present for you out here.'

"Mother said, 'Oh, bring them in, they're three days old,'

and in a minute Father came in with two, not one, but two baby lambs. They were Dolly's twins, born three days before, and they had not told us about them!

" 'An awful time to have babies, I told Dolly,' Father said, 'but I do most certainly thank you.'

" 'Oh, we most certainly thank her too,' I cried.

"And Nicky said softly: 'This is a very, very, very special Christmas.'

* * * * *

"It was a whole week before they plowed through to rescue us. We took the animals back in the bobsled that came after us. We had to leave the wagon until the next summer because it was buried in the snow. And we named the lambs Merry and Christmas, and Nicky and I each took home one of the tin stars to keep. And," Grandmother finished, "best of all we had learned that it's true: Everywhere, everywhere, Christmas tonight."

Val [Valentine] Teal was born in Bottineau, North Dakota. Besides her many short stories, she also wrote such books as *The Little Woman Wanted Noise* (1943), *Angel Child* (1946), and *It Was Not What I Expected* (1948).

The Five-O'clock Train

Ina Brevoort Roberts

Two people were waiting for the five-o'clock train that would take them to Christmas—but they were not going to the same place.

Nevertheless, they had sixty minutes together. And much can happen in sixty minutes.

How was it that Tolstoy put it? "Life can give us only moments, but for those moments we give our lives."

* * * * *

This timeless story was first published in the December 1911 issue of Woman's Home Companion.

* * * * *

Her eyes smiled a welcome as Acton joined her. "I'm glad you've come," she said; "I've grown tired of being alone."

"Alone!" Acton repeated, incredulously. They were in the largest railroad-station in the country, and around them the human tide beat insistently with a dull, unceasing roar.

"I meant what I said," she told him; and she made a picture as she said it. She was good to look at, charming and very alert. "I think a railway-station is the most 'alone' place in the world," she went on. "You see, each one's thought is in the place to which he or she is going. In the theater even, it's different; there most minds are occupied with the same thing—the play."

"That's true," Acton admitted. "I'd never thought about it before, though."

"The only exception," she continued, "is during the holidays, when everyone's heart and mind are full of Christmas and home. Then there's a silver thread of sympathy and companionship and happiness running through even a railway-station crowd."

"What time does your train leave?" he asked.

"At five."

He glanced up at the big clock, which stood at four. "It's good of you to give me this hour. Have you your ticket and your seat?"

"No, but I—there's no hurry." She was a trifle breathless, and the color had almost left her cheeks. "It will make things seem so irrevocable: the buying of that ticket. I want to put it off—a while." She glanced quickly up at Acton, and looked away again. "One must always want to pause on the threshold of a new life, I suppose. I may as well tell you: I'm going to marry John Vanwood."

Acton drew a quick breath, but gave no other sign of emotion. "He is to be congratulated," he said quietly.

"I'm to go with him on the five-o'clock train to visit his people."

The only phrases that came to Acton's mind he discarded as inane and futile. "I hope you'll be very happy," was what he said.

"I hope so too," she replied, her eyes humorous again. "One

looks for happiness from marriage more than from anything else in life. I suppose that is why there are so many doubts and uncertainties. It seems such a momentous question to decide. If one could only feel sure! I do hope I shall be able to make him happy; he's a very good man."

"I know," admitted Acton. "You will make him happy." He spoke the last words with a certain crispness to hide his deeper feeling.

"I dread this visit," she said next, with a little shiver. "I suppose a woman always does dread the thought of meeting the relatives of the man she is going to marry. They may not like me."

"They will." Acton's tone was light but sincere.

"Well, I hope so. At any rate, I'm sure I'm going to like them. Mr. Vanwood has described them to me—his mother and father, and his home. His mother is tall, with white hair and a dignified carriage, but under her real demeanor, he says, she has the kindest heart. His father is dignified too, and very handsome. I fancy Mr. Vanwood must resemble him. He's very good-looking, don't you think so?"

"Very," returned Acton stiffly. He had been assuring himself that he was no dog in the manger, and feeling grateful because he could muster magnanimity enough to admit heartily all Vanwood's worthiness. But to hear the girl he loved praise another man's looks! *Why should I be able to agree decently when she called him good, yet feel irritated when she praises his handsome face?* He asked himself.

"His people are to give a party tonight for him, a very splendid party," the girl went on. "He's been busy for the last three days telegraphing home about having plenty of roses about, and hanging the doorways with curtains of smilax. There are other delightful features that are to be surprises for me. His mother wrote me such a friendly letter, asking me to come with him." The girl was talking fast and very gaily. "Oh, it's to be a very merry party! He has a lot of brothers and sisters, and he says they'll all crowd into a big red auto and come to meet us. It seems wonderful to me—so much comfort and magnificence, all taken as a matter of course. I've never been poor, but then I've never known much luxury either. With Mr. Vanwood's people, formal dinners and motorcar rides are everyday occurrences; to me they are events." She stopped abruptly. A second later she turned to Acton with a repentant look. "I'm sorry; I've rattled on inexcusably about myself. Now tell me about *you*. You're taking a train, too?"

"Yes; I'm going home for a few days." His voice lingered lovingly on the words, but the brief silence that followed spoke of loneliness. "The only home I have, that is. When a man reaches thirty, if he hasn't a home of his own, he's really homeless."

"Tell me about them—your father and your mother and your home." Her voice was wistful. "They are all three blessings I've not known since I've been old enough to remember."

"The home is a farmhouse," began Acton obediently, "the same one to which Father took Mother when they were married. We've been fairly prosperous of late, and the house has been modernized. There are bathrooms and a telephone, and we run our own dynamo* by water-power to make the electric light. But Mother has managed somehow to keep it the same old-fashioned place. There's a living-room with big, comfortable chairs and quaint mahogany tables and a fireplace that

---

* Very few rural homes back then had access to electricity.

will hold a tree-trunk. The dining-room has a door opening out on a porch. The house is on top of a little hill; there are mountains all around it, and a glorious view with every meal."

Acton was giving all his mind to his description in an effort to forget how miserable he was; then, for a moment, his courage left him.

"Do you know that it's snowing outside?" he asked dully and irrelevantly.

"No. Is it? Go on—tell me more about your people. What are your father and mother like?"

"I don't know that I can," he replied. "They're just the best father and mother a man ever had, that's all I can say. Since I've been living in the city I've seen so many people who make a pretty poor job of parenthood that I've come nearer to appreciating them than I used to."

"They'll be glad to see you, won't they?" The girl's voice was again wistful and questioning.

He laughed. "Well, rather. You may be sure that Mother's been busy for days, baking all the things I've liked to eat from my boyhood up. She'll have sugar cookies, and molasses cookies, and doughnuts, to say nothing of pies and cakes—and salads and soups. If Mother had been born a generation later, she'd have been into all kinds of things—clubs and charities, and suffrage too, maybe. Even as it is, she has a progressive spirit; so she busies herself in keeping up to date in the same thing that occupied her in her younger days—cooking. She asked me to send her the latest and most approved cook-book, and every once in a while I ship her a boxful of fancy cooking-materials."

"How delightful!" laughed the girl. "Have you brothers and sisters, and will there be a party for you to-night?"

"No, to both questions. Tomorrow the neighbors will be driving up all day, but it would be against the unwritten etiquette of the community not to leave us alone the first evening."

"I see." After her words, gently spoken, a silence fell upon them. The stentorian tones of a trainman announcing a western express recalled Acton to himself. He looked up at the clock. Half of his precious hour was gone. He turned to the girl beside him, noting the soft curve of her throat, the way her hair grew at her temples, the exquisite lines of her lips, and the look in the eyes that mirrored her altogether satisfactory personality. Suddenly there came from his lips the last words he had intended to say to her.

"I wish," he said, "that you were coming home with *me*, and that I could tell them you were going to marry me. I ought not to say this, I suppose, and yet—there can be no wrong in your knowing that I love you."

He paused, but she did not speak. "I've been thinking about it," he went on, "the wonder of it, if you were going with me. It would be very different, though, altogether different from the kind of good time you're going to have, and, I suppose, not nearly so satisfactory. Father would meet us with a sleigh, and one thing would be quite as beautiful—the ride home."

"There are few things more enchanting than the right kind of snow-storm," said the girl gravely.

"Well, we have the right kind up there." He forced cheerfulness into his tone. "When we arrived, Mother would kiss you, and she and Father and I would take off your wraps. After supper we'd establish you comfortably before the living-room fire."

"I know the rest of the story," interrupted the girl. "All the

while your father and mother were setting me at ease they'd be mentally appraising me to see if I were worthy of you. And when the tree-trunk had become a mass of embers your father would light my candle,—I'm sure, in spite of the electric lights, there are candles,—and your mother would go with me to my room. There she and I would have a little talk and then—"

"And then," finished Acton, "she would come downstairs and tell me it was all right and that you would do."

"Are you sure that is what she would say?"

"Absolutely. What will *really* happen, though, is that, after my light is out, Mother will come and sit on the edge of my bed, and I shall tell her about you; and she will wonder how any girl can have the poor taste to prefer any man in the world to me!" ended Acton with a laugh that, in spite of his effort, sounded mirthless.

In the silence that followed, the tramp of countless footsteps on the stone floor, the murmur of voices reverberating throughout the lofty dome, all the sounds of restless waiting and hurrying humanity, sounded dim and distant to Acton. He was wondering if she had forgiven his outburst. He wanted her to think well of him in the years to come, years that she was to live as another man's wife. *Another man's wife!* The words burned in his brain.

"How long have you been engaged?" he asked in a sudden attempt to get back to conventional, safe-to-be-talked-about topics.

"I—I—why, we're not really engaged at all yet. He asked me a week ago, but of course I had to have time to consider so momentous a question. So we arranged that, if my answer were to be 'Yes,' I was to meet him here in time for the five-o'clock train, and go home with him. He would take my non-appearance as meaning that my answer would be 'No.'"

"He ought to be here soon; it's getting close to five," Acton said.

"He told me he could not come till the last moment," the girl responded.

Once more Acton glanced at the clock. "Well, we still have ten minutes." He had not looked at her, but he could feel in every nerve all her charm and sweetness.

She seemed about to speak when another train announcer's voice, close to their ears, startled them both. When the man had walked away again, she said:

"That was a beautiful picture you drew—of your homecoming. I shall always remember it." He felt rather than saw that she too was nervously watching the clock. He knew now, by the gentle note in her voice, that she had forgiven him, and he supposed she was going on to tell him how sorry she was, and all the miserable et cetera that went with such speeches.

"But," she breathed, "I couldn't go with you—to-day. Why, they wouldn't be expecting me."

Tolstoy once said, "Life can give us only moments, but for those moments we give our lives." It was one of these moments that came now to Acton, an instant almost unbearable in its deep happiness. But realization of his joy would keep, he told himself with a quick gathering of his mental forces; action was needed now.

"That wouldn't make any difference—the fact that they do not expect you. I'm all they have in the world, so there isn't any preparation they could make that they haven't made just for me. And in Mother's last letter she said she had hoped that before this I would be bringing my wife home. A fiancée is the

next best thing to a wife, isn't she? Will you come?"

He turned to her, and their eyes met. The look in hers was frankly glad.

"Yes, I'll come. Oh, I know now why I felt so doubtful and uncertain before. How good it is to be *sure!*"

All that he wanted to do and say Acton had to put into the look he gave her. "We'll have to hurry," he whispered as he took up her bag, and together they ran toward the five-o'clock train.

Ina Brevoort Roberts was born in 1874, in Yonkers, New York. Besides her many short stories, she also wrote *The Lifting of a Finger* in 1901.

Christmas Bell

Adeline Rumsey

Christmas at wartime. People everywhere uprooted, migrating to wherever factories needed workers. Women too—with so many men away at the front, and with so many other men in war-related research and logistical support—everyone was needed.

But Nancy was lonely—lonely for her hometown far away.

Then—an overshoe zipper stuck.

* * * * *

She had been hanging a red paper bell on the chandelier in the living-room when the doorbell rang. She stood in the open doorway while she read the telegram the boy had brought; she read it over twice and it still said the same thing:

ARRIVING SATURDAY MORNING 7:30 WITH BABY. PLEASE GET EVERYTHING. MARIE

Down in the corner, just to make sure that it was clear, the "7:30" had been retyped. They needn't have bothered doing that, Nancy thought. The "7:30" part was clear enough; what they should have retyped was "with baby."

With baby. Marie, her sister, and Tom, her brother-in-law, had gone to Chicago to talk with an agency about adopting a baby. And they were coming back with the baby. On Christmas. At seven-thirty in the morning.

"They can't," Nancy said.

The telegraph boy, who was only halfway down the steps, turned around and looked at her.

"They just can't," Nancy said. "Not so quickly."

He looked rather more alarmed than interested. He said in a cautious tone, "You say something, Miss?"

Nancy took her eyes off the telegram long enough to notice that he was staring at her and that she was talking to herself. She said, almost with dignity, "I said Merry Christmas. Here," and gave him two quarters from the pile of them that Marie always kept on the table by the door at Christmas time. The boy said, "Thanks! Merry Christmas!" Nancy said Merry Christmas twice more and then found that she was smiling foolishly. She stepped back into the house and slammed the door behind her, laughing at herself. She looked up at the paper bell and gave it a derisive whack with her hand and said, "We don't need you to make it a merry one! We've got a baby coming!"

* * * * *

The bell had been a symbol, a compromise. A feeble attempt at Christmas cheer. She had bought the bell and hung it up because it seemed too hard to have Tom and Marie coming in from Chicago on Christmas Eve, tired and bleak, and to have not even one sign of Christmas in the little rented house. Marie had said before they went that nothing they could do would make it seem like Christmas this year and so why bother? "We can't have a tree anyway," she said, "because all the ornaments are in storage. And it won't be Christmas without a tree, and anyway it won't be Christmas. Not here."

But up and down the street it was going to be Christmas; Nancy could tell. She had seen the trees carried in, she had seen the children delivering presents, she had seen the grocer-boys with their huge boxes. She had heard the muffled whir of vacuum cleaners as rooms were cleaned and polished and cleaned again. In imagination she had heard the slap-slap of wooden spoons beating out cake batter in yellow bowls. All up and down the street it would be Christmas; it wasn't right not to celebrate it, even if you were living in a furnished house in a strange town where you had no friends at all.

They had moved there, she and Tom and Marie, just three months before. She had been living with them at the time; acute appendicitis after months of overwork had sent her home from her job in Washington with doctor's orders to take life easy for at least six months. At first it had seemed like a dream come true—a chance to spend six months at home, resting, enjoying life and seeing her old friends. Then one night Tom had come home from the shop with a thunderbolt in his hands and had dropped it calmly into their laps. They were moving. They were leaving the town where they had grown up and going to another that they had never even heard of. They would probably stay there as long as the war might last.

"Because that's where I'm needed, Marie," he kept saying. "You do understand that, don't you?"

Marie had understood, and she had been a good sport about it. She had rented her house and put her own things in storage, and she and Nancy had stayed in a hotel at first and searched through the town for a livable house during the first weeks while Tom got used to his new job.

Nancy had been grateful for the appendix that had sent

her home to be with Marie at just that time because only she knew how hard it was for her sister. Only she knew quite how desolate Marie had to be before she would say, "Let's not bother with Christmas."

Because the months they had spent there had been lonely. Worse than lonely. Bewildered and ineffectual. They had met a few people of course—mostly preoccupied wives of men who, like Tom, worked at the plant. They had bowing acquaintances now with all the neighbors; they called good morning to them brightly. "But how do you get to know them?" Marie would say. "How do you make real friends? *I* don't know."

She had never had to make new friends in her life. She didn't know how to begin. And Nancy was sorry to see that she didn't intend even to try to find out. Instead she had turned in on herself; she spent most of her time in the house, cleaning it until it shone, reading, writing letters to her friends at home. She was doing nothing but wait for the day when she could move back there. And in the meantime she was unhappy. Nancy had been really worried about her.

For Nancy it was not so much of a problem. In a month or two she would be strong again and she would be going away. Back to Washington, perhaps, to take up her work again. But it was hard to think that she would have to leave Marie like this—to leave her so downhearted that she hadn't wanted even to celebrate Christmas.

The only thing Marie had done since the work of settling was over was to redouble her efforts to find the baby that she and Tom had wanted for so long to adopt—ever since they had known that there wouldn't be any young Toms running around unless they did adopt them. They had always intended to adopt a baby someday. Now that they were here Marie had

gone at it as energetically as though it were all that mattered. In three months nothing whatsoever had happened; nothing except two wild goose chases, many letters reminding them that it took patience, and one interview which they had finally been able to arrange for December twenty-third. To have to be on a train on Christmas Eve had seemed to Nancy like an extra misery for them. So she had bought a turkey—a big one—and baked a mince pie and made Christmas candy. She had bought the big red bell and hung it in the living-room. And all of it was so that when Tom and Marie came home tired and discouraged on Christmas Eve they would find waiting at least some sign of Christmas.

But they weren't coming home on Christmas Eve. They wouldn't be back until Christmas morning—and they were bringing a baby.

* * * * *

"So," Nancy said to the bell, "we'd better get busy." She walked through the living-room so fast that her passing sent up air currents that set the bell to whirling; it was still whirling gaily when she snatched her hat and went out. It was five-thirty already. The stores would stay open until nine-thirty because it was Christmas Eve, but from five-thirty to nine-thirty on Christmas Eve is not much time for shopping, especially when you have to stop for everything that a baby needs. It had begun to snow a little, which was a nuisance; she whirled in her tracks, rushed in and out of the house in the same motion and was out on the path again with her overshoes in her hand. When Nancy hurried she did it right; she was like a small tornado blowing itself through the streets. She carried

her overshoes to the corner and plumped down on the curb to put them on. She had to wait for a trolley-car and she didn't want to miss it. She might as well be fastening her overshoes while she waited.

It was dark already, with the quick cold darkness of a day that was nearly the shortest day of the year, and she hardly noticed the tall thin figure until he stood over her. Somebody else waiting for the car of course; that must mean that it would be along soon. She tugged with extra impatience at the overshoe, concentrating so that she didn't even look up when he said, "Can I help you?"

"It's the third snap," Nancy said. "Can't get zippers any more and the darned thing always sticks."

"I mean," he said, "can I help you up? I thought you had slipped."

"Oh no," Nancy said, "I'm just in a hurry—oh dear, there it is! The car!"

"The third snap?" he said and knelt down suddenly. His hands reached for the overshoe deliberately, without hurrying. As the car rocked down the track toward them, he fastened it. He had it done at exactly the right moment; he caught Nancy's hand and pulled her to her feet with one hand, hailed the car and reached in his pocket for change with the other. They were sitting on the long straw-covered seat in the warm brightly lighted trolley before she had time to do more than realize that the third snap wasn't stuck anymore.

She blinked her eyes against the lights, looking into his face, and said, "Why, hello. I know you, don't I?"

"That's right," he said. "I'm your next-door neighbor, three times removed."

"I know—wait a minute—you're—" She closed her eyes tight, trying to remember. Was he the Mr. Weems who had the cute twin boys or was he the newly married Mr. Warner whose young wife stayed in bed until eleven o'clock and then got up looking the way every woman wants to?

"I'm Ted Miles," he said, "and I board with Mrs. Carter on the corner. I work where your brother-in-law works—where most of us work around here. Only your brother-in-law and I happen to work right in the same department, so we see each other every day."

"Of course!" she said. "That's how I met you. I would have known if I hadn't been in such a hurry." With a polite effort at making conversation she said, "You must be a chemical engineer too. Like Tom."

"I am," he said and smiled. "Though not quite like Tom. I wish I were. And why are you in such a hurry on Christmas Eve? Aren't we supposed to begin to relax about this time on Christmas Eve? Work all over, tree all trimmed, don't have to get up early tomorrow—at least, not if you're a bachelor like me, though as a matter of fact Mrs. Carter's kids will probably have me up by seven—well anyway, aren't we supposed to relax? Come on now, try it—just take a deep breath—one, two, three, relax!"

* * * * *

He gave the command like a drill sergeant. Nancy, laughing, said, "But I can't relax! I've got loads of shopping to do."

"That's downright unpatriotic," he said. "You mean you've still got to get those foot-warmers for Aunt Sally? And wrap them up and everything, and load the mails with them? Or are they for next Christmas?"

"Not Christmas shopping," she said. "Don't tease me, I'm not a bit good at it. It's not Christmas shopping, but I have to do it tonight or bust. I've got to buy a baby carriage." And then, before his astonished eyes, she pulled the telegram out of her pocket and showed it to him.

"Is it a gag?" he said at last.

"Of course not. They've wanted a baby for years and now they've found one to adopt. I'm so pleased for them I could choke." Looking at his face, she saw the smile begin to break over it. He was dark and his face was thin and solemn. She knew that Tom had referred to him as one of the bright boys, and she knew what Tom meant by it, how much Tom thought of him. She knew that in back of the high forehead there was such knowledge and intelligence that Tom admired and spoke of him; that he was indispensable at the plant, so that there had never been a question about where he should be in wartime. Ordinarily he looked serious enough for his responsibilities. When he smiled now, though, his face was split in two, split right in the middle by the small boy that used to live there. His smile was merry, carefree, young and infectious.

He said, "May I come too? It's been ages since I've had to shop for a baby carriage."

She smiled back at him and shopping for the baby became a lark.

* * * * *

"Now the first thing you do," he said, "is map your campaign."

They had dinner together; a quick meal in a shiny cafeteria in the shopping district. Outside the window they could see the crowds going by, tired but merry. The restaurant door opened constantly, letting in wave after wave of shoppers, each of them wrapped in an invisible cloak of the cold clear Christmasy air. The snow had stopped, but you could still smell it and feel it and be refreshed by it. The shoppers brought it in with them, the way they brought their bundles. They put their bundles down on the tables and lowered themselves into their chairs as though they were putting down a heavy burden, but in a few minutes they would begin poking at the bundles, touching each one lovingly, tearing a tiny hole to peer in at some treasure.

Nancy noticed, without meaning to, how many people knew Ted. They called to him happily, the way people do when they have seen each other only a short time before and know that they will see each other soon again. They made some laughing allusion, the key to which she did not have, and then, seeing her with him, bowed and smiled politely. It was like looking in at a club where she was not a member and was not wanted. They were such a close little group, these people here in the town. Just like the group at home, really— except that she and Marie didn't belong. And at home they had been at the very heart of it.

The baby was coming tomorrow, she reminded herself, and then they would be a group all by themselves. Not lonely. Not lost. Not exiles. The baby would come and after that never mind all these people who weren't friends, although they were friendly. They could get along fine without them.

"That's right," she said. "We map our campaign. Where do we start? Bottles? Carriage? Diapers?"

"In alphabetical order," Ted said, "just as you've said." He tore a leaf from a notebook and made a quick list of the

alphabet down one side. "We'll skip A, because the most important thing is under B. Baby first. Your sister and brother-in-law are supplying that. Now then—what else?"

"Bottles," said Nancy. "Bathinette. Bunny. To play with."

"Bunny, to play with," he wrote. "C. Crib, carriage, clothes."

"Let's see—D. Diapers, dish, doll—no, she's too young for a doll—wait a minute, maybe she's not even a she! All right, skip the doll. E. F—food." Her eyes grew wide as she stared at him. "Food. Ration points!"*

"Let's just put that under M," he said. "Milk. Come on, keep going, we haven't much time. Under N?"

"Nothing."

"Nothing," he wrote intently. "O, P—play pen. Babies don't need much, do they? We've got lots of empty letters."

Somewhere between N, for nothing, and P, for play pen, however, they realized that babies did need rather a lot. The worst of it was that nothing could be delivered before next week at the earliest. Especially the more important items—the crib, carriage, the bathinette. They were hard enough to find at all, the clerk said, and you always had to wait for them.

"Though I do have one carriage," she added. "It's a closeout. Slightly damaged. But we couldn't deliver it of course."

Ted Miles looked thoughtful. "You couldn't deliver it—but could we take it?"

She looked surprised. "Why—I suppose so."

"We'll take it," Ted said. "Now."

They took it. They paid for it. They tied their sales slip to the top of the hood, so that nobody would think they were stealing it. They pushed it through the crowded aisles, asking pardons right and left as the shoppers moved out of their way. Nearly everybody smiled at them; nearly everybody was interested. It turned, in the end, into a sort of triumphal procession through the baby department. Bottles, a bunny, diapers, a dish. Shirts and sweaters and nightgowns and safety pins and rattles—they bought whatever they had for babies that would fit into the carriage.

"We can't get the bathinette," Nancy said looking worriedly at the list. "Nor the crib—but she can sleep in the carriage, I guess. And we can't get the high chair, but that's all right because we can hold her on our laps for a while; and we can't get the play pen, but we can just put a blanket on the floor till she gets to the crawling stage—oh dear! There's such a lot we can't get."

Ted had moved a few feet away to look at a display of bootees; the clerk said sympathetically, "You'll find everything, it just takes time." And then added softly, "When's the baby coming?"

"Tomorrow," Nancy said happily.

They were still laughing at the look on her face when they went out of the store into the crowded street. They laughed their way through the shower of Merry Christmases that followed them now wherever they pushed their absurdly laden carriage. Packages filled every inch of it; packages were tied to the hood, to the handle, to the springs.

"We'll have to walk home," Nancy said. "We can't get this into a taxi." For some reason it was a special private joke.

When they were nearly home, it began to snow again—lightly, melting as it fell. A woman waiting for a bus glared after them; they heard her say, too loudly, "I call it wicked

---

* In war time, food was rationed.

have a baby out on a night like this!" Their laughter at that took them all the way home.

* * * * *

Some of the laughter was still left in her when she stood in the station the next morning. She had been up till nearly two, opening the packages, putting things away; Ted Miles had stayed with her, helping her move another bureau into the spare room, helping her carry the carriage up the stairs, helping her decide where the baby should sleep so as to be out of the draft and still get air enough. She had got up again after only a few hours' sleep, long before it was light; put coal on the furnace herself, made sure the house would be warm enough and the breakfast would be ready. She had dressed and stuffed the turkey, getting him all ready to pop in the oven—"For you'll have to cook yourself," she said to him firmly. "We won't have time for you."

She should have been tired and she should have been cold, waiting for the train in the dimly lighted station, but while she waited she felt only laughter and excitement and joy.

Then there they were. Tom and Marie. And she was looking at them and looking at something they had with them—something they had with them—something that seemed to consist of two blue eyes peering out of a pink bunting. In that moment she found that her throat had closed up all of a sudden; her throat and her chest were full of an emotion that was so big it didn't allow expression of any kind—not laughter, nor tears, nor words. She could only reach for the baby and take hold of the bunting thing and stare; after a minute she said distractedly, "Why, Marie! She's beautiful!"

"*He's* tired," Marie said. "He looks a great deal better when he's rested. He's really very handsome." She tugged at the hood of the bunting, changing its position by a full sixteenth of an inch.

"You can tell more about him when he's out of that bunting thing," Tom said. "Here, Rie, let me take him. Takes a man to carry a weight like that."

"I'll carry him, thank you," Marie said crisply. "He's used to me. Come on, let's go, he should have had his orange juice by this time." She looked like a little girl, playing with a doll and pretending to be grown up, trotting along so importantly with her heavy bundle. Tom was almost strutting beside her.

In the taxi, out of the jumble of conversation a few facts came out. "He's five months old. . . . He was born July fourth, isn't that wonderful? . . . He's been at the Home all this time. . . . He's getting a tooth—look, there. No, silly, the lower ones come first—look, down there—"

"What's his name?" Nancy asked.

"AhGoo. At least, that's what he keeps saying when we ask him. Well, here we are." Marie looked out of the taxi window, stared at the house and made a little face. "Somehow I thought it might have changed," she said. "Well, no matter. Come along, AhGoo."

When they got inside, she did not notice the red bell that hung from the chandelier. Neither she nor Tom had any attention left over from looking at the baby. But Nancy felt rewarded anyway for hanging the bell, for the baby saw it. He lay on his back on the couch and smiled benignly every now and then as though to encourage them. But most of the time he stared happily at the bell as it twirled slowly in the air currents. When somebody walked through the room the bell circled faster; once Tom caught Marie by the waist and they waltzed

for a minute in the middle of the room, while the bell whirled like mad and the baby laughed.

* * * * *

It wasn't half-past eight when the doorbell rang the first time. Ted Miles was standing on the porch stamping the snow from his overshoes and supporting an oversized package behind him.

He said, "Good morning, did you ever try to tie up one of these in red tissue paper?"

Nancy said, "Ted! How nice!" And then for no reason at all she turned quite pink and could find nothing else to say. Tom went forward to greet Ted Miles, and nobody paid any attention to Marie. But then Ted said, "Nancy and I practically supplied your child's trousseau, you know, though she may not have had a chance to tell you about it. So I came around this morning to say congratulations—many of them. And many merry Christmases. And now the question is—" he shifted his burden— "and, incidentally, Mrs. Carter and I have discussed this question since six-fifteen—the question is, is he a morning-bath baby or is he an evening-bath baby? Because if he's a morning-bath baby I'm just in time, but if he's an evening-bath baby I could have let you have your breakfast in peace."

"He's a morning-bath baby," Marie said, "and we've had breakfast."

"Then I'm just in time," Ted said and whipped his package around from behind his back, opened it with a flourish and a great crackling of tissue paper, and set it up in the middle of the floor.

"A bathinette," he said as though he had kept it a secret.

"Mrs. Carter says Billy's grown too big for it."

"But how wonderful!" Nancy said. "And I was so upset because we couldn't get one!"

Marie said, "How kind of her! Please tell her thank you! And I'll come over to say it in person when I get a chance."

"You needn't bother," Ted said. "I give her until twenty past nine to get here. That's as long as she's ever been known to wait to see a new baby in the neighborhood."

* * * * *

It was exactly nineteen minutes past nine when Mrs. Carter got there. She came in through the back door, and she brought a box of cookies. She put them down on the kitchen table and said, "It's just some cookies. Mizz Wallace is coming over later with the cake—but I thought these would be nice to have out, you know, when the folks get to coming—is that your bird? Oh honey, you ought to have him in the oven this minute; he's a big one. What time you going to eat? Twelve?"

"We hadn't planned any time," Nancy said. "We thought we'd eat whenever we were hungry; there are just the three of us. Thank you so much for the cookies and I can't tell you how we feel about the bathinette—oh dear, was that the doorbell?"

"You go answer it," Mrs. Carter said, "and I'll get the turkey in—here, give me your apron. Yes, it'll reach around—who's that at the back door? Oh, it's just Evie Wallace with the cake—you go ahead. I'll tend to the bird."

Nancy went ahead. She went, systematically, between the front door and the back door. She shuttled between the kitchen and the living-room. Every minute all morning, it seemed, there was a neighbor opening the back door and

86

putting something down on the table and standing to talk for a while with Mrs. Carter.

"I never saw anything like it," Nancy said once incredulously, stopping for a minute to stare at the cookies and cakes, the plum puddings and candies, the jellies and rolls that stood on the kitchen table and overflowed onto the stool and the leaf of the cabinet and the top of the icebox. "I never saw anything like it."

"The food, you mean?" Mrs. Carter said, "Oh, we always do that." She was sitting before the hot stove; she fanned herself with Nancy's apron and looked complacently at the loaded table. "That's country style, you know. Any time there's a death or a birth—you know, something like that. Any time there's anything going on, the neighbors always help out. There's a lot of extra company and you need things."

"I know," Nancy said dazedly, "but just at Christmas, when you're all so busy—oh! Your own turkey! Your own Christmas! And here you are bothering about us!"

Mrs. Carter looked more complacent still. "My kids are just the right age," she said. "The youngest one's young enough so they've all been up since the dawn, and we've had most of our Christmas. Besides, the oldest one's old enough so she ought to know how to baste a turkey, or I'll baste her. But I might be getting home, at that."

After she left Nancy stood thoughtfully looking at the party food on the table. Enough cookies for a regiment. And they knew nobody in town. Then she went to the door of the living-room, looked in, and counted. There were nine people. While she watched the doorbell rang again and then there were twelve.

Nobody came empty-handed. Not many of the things they brought were new, but they were all useful. Those things that had seemed unobtainable last night appeared as if by magic; there was a high chair, there was a play pen, there was a large basket that would do until a crib could be had. There were clothes and extra diapers, and toys of every sort up to and including a baseball bat.

In the middle of it Nancy noticed that Ted Miles had gone; she found him half an hour later, trying to sneak in the back door with two Christmas trees—one so big he had to drag it, the other a tiny one for the baby's room. He was followed by three small Carter children carrying boxes of ornaments left over from the Carter tree and from eighteen years of stationary married life. Half an hour later, when they had just settled down to the trimming, Tom came lumbering in the front door with two Christmas trees—one so big he had to drag it, the other a tiny one for the baby's room. The Carter children went out foraging for more ornaments and they set up all four trees and trimmed them all.

Somehow, around two o'clock, they served their turkey and ate it. And just in time, for in the afternoon the real rush began. Nancy, answering the constantly ringing doorbell, knew there were lots of repeaters; she could tell them by the way they viewed the baby, as though they already owned a good big share of him and were proud to show him off to those who hadn't seen him that morning.

Nancy found herself late in the afternoon, wedged into a corner with Ted Miles, eating one of Mrs. Carter's Christmas cookies. She said, around the raisins, "It's wonderful. I never saw anything like it."

He smiled at her. "I know. The people in this town have something, haven't they?"

87

Too many cookies and too much turkey and too much company made extra words seem foolish; she found that she was saying, boldly, things she wouldn't have admitted yesterday. She said, "I'm so glad for Marie. I think she'll like the place better after this. She's hated it so far."

"Has she?" he said. He didn't look surprised. "Everybody does at first."

Words were too much trouble but her eyes questioned him.

He said, looking around the room, "Mrs. Carter, now—she never hated it, because she's always lived here. And Mrs. Wallace and two or three others. Then you get to Mrs. Bryan, for instance—why, she's an old inhabitant. Been here a year." He smiled at her expression. "We're all exiles, you know—if you want to use that word. None of us lived here before. We're all brought here by the same thing. Our work." His face was serious now.

"So we're at home, really," he said. "And we're together. Working for our country."

Nancy took a deep breath. "You make it sound so good. I hadn't thought—"

He smiled. "It doesn't just sound good. It is good. Look at Marie now."

* * * * *

Nancy looked across the room. She saw Marie sitting on the couch, holding AhGoo on her lap. She was discussing formulas with Mrs. Bryan while Mrs. Carter measured his left foot for bootees and knitted.

She said, "I know. It makes everything different you know—I would have hated to leave her here, the way things were."

"Leave her?" he said.

"When I go, I mean. Back to work."

"Back to work?" he said. He picked up one of Mrs. Carter's cookies; he weighed it in his hand. He said, "We've a plant here, you know. We need workers."

"Here?" her astonishment was genuine; she had never thought of staying here herself. And then, in one minute, the astonishment was gone completely.

"Because," he said, "after all, we've got something here." He smiled. "AhGoo for instance."

She smiled back at him. Around them the babel of voices went on. Over in the corner somebody turned the radio on; a chorus from *The Messiah* came ringing out of it; the words were loud and clear: "For unto us a child is born, unto us a son is given—"

Nancy looked across the room at the baby. He lay on the couch looking up; looking beyond the friendly faces that crowded around him, looking behind the people who had come to welcome him. He looked at the bell that hung above their heads, the cheap Christmas bell made out of paper. "Ah-Goo," said the baby and the bell whirled.

Adeline Rumsey Hendrix (1865–1944) was born in Tompkins County, New York. She wrote for popular magazines during the late nineteenth and first half of the twentieth centuries.

Christmas Eve

Kathleen Coyle

What on earth could a little boy singing a Christmas carol outside a dark corner near a railway station have to do with a broken-hearted woman in a cheap apartment?

* * * * *

The boy curled up in the deep chair by the window was so engrossed in his reading that he did not notice how the daylight was going until the door opened and his mother came in with her arms full of paper bags and packages. She let in with her a strong illuminating ray from the electric bulb in the corridor. It searched her out and revealed her to him clearly as she headed for the cubbyhole that was their kitchen.

At that instant their opposite neighbor, Mrs. Patchielli, came across and stood silhouetted on their threshold. "That you, Nelly? My, you look as though you were going to celebrate. Did you get a tree?"

Jake saw his mother turn. She hesitated an instant; then she said, her voice a wisp of dryness, "No . . . and I'm not going to."

Mrs. Patchielli made the queer little sound that always came from her by way of protest. "Now! Now! Last year you acted the same. You didn't have a tree. I was new then. It puzzled me. Now I know you. But what's wrong? Something to do with your husband? Something that . . . hurts?"

You couldn't stop Momma Patchielli once she got going, except with the truth. In the tiny kitchen, Nelly March moved her face out of the light. "Yes," she admitted. "Burch walked out on me on Christmas Eve. He had brought in a tree . . ."

"That's bad," Mrs. Patchielli said. "Things shouldn't go wrong on birthdays or feast days so that you can't ever forget."

"It was my fault. I started the quarrel. It was after the operation when I lost my baby. Every cent had to be counted. Jake was only four at the time. We were living over Flack's the florist's down by the depot. Burch got the tree in Flack's and came up with it. Then . . ." She choked. She added, "It was all my fault. He went. He never came back. Then I moved here. I got a job."

"How do you know he never came back?"

"Because he'd have found me. Trayton isn't a big place. Listen. I don't want to . . . remember." She went into the living room and switched on the light.

Jake jumped up out of the chair, blinking. "Wow!" he exclaimed.

His mother said, "Jake! I thought you were down at the clubhouse practicing carols."

He was pulling on his mackinaw in a hurry. "Oops, Mom, I forgot." He was gone in a blue streak.

* * * * *

It was Christmas Eve. The night was cold. It was snowing, but the white flakes melted as they fell. The ground was slushy. People were going about with umbrellas. But in spite of the misery of the weather, the carol singers were doing well.

They were collecting for their club, which had a tree and was going to have a turkey dinner for kids whose fathers were out of work.

It was late when Jake suddenly demanded that they should sing in front of Flack's the florist's. The whole gang was against the suggestion: what would they get down in that dark corner by the railway depot? Jake insisted. He was the youngest in the bunch, but he had magnificent bargaining powers, because he was their soprano. It was his voice that brought in the pennies, opened pocketbooks, and moved the hearts of all who listened. He told them he wanted to get a tree at Flack's. "I want to get a tree for my mom," he pleaded.

So they gave in, and down they went and planted themselves on the sidewalk before Flack's. The snow was coming down white. On the steps by the florist's window, the trees that were still unsold were stacked. Jake kept his eyes on them. He had an ambition that was as unstoppable as Mrs. Patchielli's kindness. They sang "Come All Ye Merry Gentlemen," "Good King Wenceslaus," and "Holy Night." It was Jake's treble that took the sweetness of the Holy Night out upon the dark little deserted corner. Windows opened. A few stragglers came down the side street or up from the railway. A man stopped and waited while the boy's notes rang their pure bells in the air. Jake saw him. He sang to him. He remembered dimly a big man who used to take him up on his shoulders. He sang as though the notes went from him right up to God. He wished his dad would come back. He wished he had never gone away. He remembered how, a long time ago, he had found his mother sobbing, lying on the bed with her face in the blankets. He would take her home a tree.

When he stopped singing, the boys made the collection

and the man on the step came right over to him and gave him a dollar. "Thank you, son," he said.

"Son?" Jake repeated. "My father went away."

The man peered down at him, studying the boy from his red hair to the stubbed shoes.

And then, with childlike abruptness, Jake blurted out, "I have to get Mom a tree."

"Good idea," the man said. "Come in here with me." They went into Flack's together, and the man chose the biggest and best tree in the shop, and paid for it. The man said, "You lead the way and I'll follow." He hoisted the tree up so that he seemed taller than ever with its crest towering over his hat.

Jake was in a trance of joy. He wanted his mom to be happy. He marched on with the man, and when they came to his home he led the way upstairs and pushed the door open. "Mom!" he cried out. "I've got you a tree!" His voice was excited.

Then he saw that something was happening to his mother. Her face had a sort of light in it. He saw the man put the tree down, against the wall. He saw him put out his arms. He heard him say, "Nelly, I came back. I had to. I came all the way from Oregon . . . I . . . want you to forgive me . . ."

He heard his mother say, very low, very deep, with something in her voice that made you want to cry, "It was my fault, Burch. I found out . . . when you didn't come back."

He heard the tree trying to move its tied branches, trying to put out its arms. And then his eyes were blurred, and the big man in the center of the floor was holding him tight against him with one arm and holding his mother tight with the other, and, away down in him, silent, he could feel the song of the Holy Night singing to him inside. Christmas had come. It had come—home.

Kathleen Coyle (1886–1952) was born in Derry, Ireland. During her busy and unorthodox lifetime, she lived in many places: Ireland, London, Antwerp, Paris, New Hampshire, Princeton, and Philadelphia. She wrote thirteen novels and many short stories (a number set during World War II). Among her friends were Rebecca West and James Joyce.

Appointment in the Desert

Margaret Cousins

At first the doctor failed to realize just how slippery the slopes of his life had become, nor how far and fast had been his descent. Then the awful realization that he'd lost everything: medical reputation, moral collapse, property, friendships, and wife.

So, not long before Christmas, he packed up, headed east, aimlessly wandering, imploring God to somehow save him from the abyss.

And then, way out in the New Mexico desert—

* * * * *

About the middle of December, John Quincy Wallace, M.D., came to the end of his tether. When he left the impressive rented house in Beverly Hills he had occupied for four years, he did not look back. After he had got into the flashy convertible and was driving through the sunny back streets of Los Angeles, under the dry, rustling palms, he realized that he did not know where he was going.

He thought, inevitably, of Sandra, his wife. He had not seen her since August—the evening they came home from the Farraguts' barbecue and Sandra said she was through—she couldn't stand it another minute. He had told her to act her age.

"All right, I will," Sandra stormed. "I'm a grown woman. You're a perpetual adolescent!"

"What do you want?" he demanded furiously. "I've given you everything money can buy."

"I want to be really married," Sandra said. "I want a home and everything we've planned—not this phony make-believe. I want to act natural."

"Once a hick, always a hick!"

"Maybe," she said, her large brown eyes streaming. "But I don't like to be pawed, and I can't bear to watch you being pawed by that little creature with the chewed-off hair. What's her name? June Moon or something!"

"Now we come to the crux of the matter."

"All right," she said. "Maybe I *am* acting natural, for a change."

"You'll feel better in the morning," he told her. "Take a sleeping pill."

"I believe I'll lie awake," Sandra said, "and see if I have forgotten how to think."

"Suit yourself," he said, and stamped off to take a dose of his own medicine.

(The next day she said she was getting out.)

* * * * *

It was very orderly; she rarely indulged in dramatics. She was a doctor's wife, and in spite of the razzle-dazzle existence they had been leading since John had been retained by one of the picture companies as a studio doctor, she had clung to the shreds of her dignity. She had been born in Kansas, as he had, but while the war had inevitably sophisticated him, she had remained much the same . . . a leaf-brown girl, small and rounded, with a tumble of bronzed hair and enormous eyes. She was a good little thing—good mind, good heart, good manners.

It was her goodness that had attracted him to her. He had had ideals of his own. His medical education had been achieved through struggle and sacrifice—his parents' and his own. Sandra's, too. They had been so terribly in love they had married when his internship was still before him. She had gone on working, making do, for years. He remembered the series of little hovels they had set up housekeeping in—mean little basement apartments or city walk-ups—and the way she had always scrubbed them out and fixed them up and made them home. She never complained, but he wanted something nice for her—a decent place to live, and pretty clothes. But he was going to revolutionize medicine, and she was going to help him.

Now, he felt hangdog when he looked at her. Without wishing it, she had become his conscience. He was aware that the tools of his trade, welded in struggle and whetted in a bloody war, were going to rust, like farm machinery left out in the rain. He was rarely called on to heal anything more important than hangovers, tantrums, or the vagaries of insomnia.

Well, the war was to blame. It was due to his meeting with the big producer in the South Pacific that he had entered on this path. The man had been babbling with malaria and attached more importance

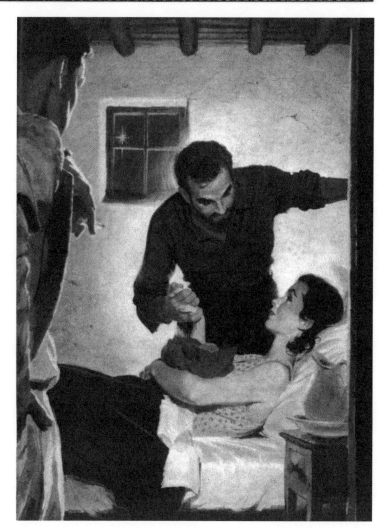

to John's administration of Atabrine than was realistic.

* * * * *

"John," Sandra said that momentous morning, "I have to go."

"A change will do you good."

"If you want a divorce, I'll give it to you."

"You're wrought up," he said. "After you've calmed down we'll talk things over. Why don't you run over to Palm Springs for a few days?"

"I'm going to Kansas," Sandra said.

"Back to the farm!"

"I don't know where else to go," Sandra told him. "I don't think a place has anything to do with it. It's the person who makes or breaks his own life."

"You'll be back," he said.

"I don't think so," she answered sadly.

"What do you expect me to do?" he demanded. "Give up $50,000 a year for one of your silly whims?"

"I don't expect anything," Sandra said. "Not now."

* * * * *

At first he had experienced relief. He enjoyed his loneliness and lack of responsibility and the skylarking that went with it ... idle days, busy evenings. He rationalized her absence with various subterfuges and threw himself into the pursuit of pleasure. As a pseudo-bachelor, presentable and well-heeled, he had no difficulties. He had the craggy profile and stiff brush of black hair that made him appear more youthful than he was, and the rugged body of a Kansas farm boy. Women always noticed him. He indulged in a few mild flirtations and began to get his name in the gossip columns, alongside the stars. This pleased rather than irritated him.

He had one letter from Sandra. She was back in Milburn and had taken a job in the post office. He answered it and sent her a check, but she did not acknowledge his letter in any way. After that, he had his office forward her regular allowance until he began to be strapped for cash. When he thought of the limitations of the little prairie town, he couldn't understand how she bore it.

She had been gone two or three months when things began to fall apart.

The couple gave notice, and he could not find anybody else who compared to the Plimmers. He had a series of indifferent servants, all of whom seemed slattern or dishonest. The house began to lose its luster. He hated to go home, and spent more and more time away.

His indulgences resulted in mounting fatigue, which he stemmed with alcohol and other sedatives. He began to get careless about office hours and the few duties that were imposed on him. Extravagance shortened his bank account, and he took to the gambling tables in Nevada now and then, trying to recoup. His latest girl—a neurotic starlet whose professional radiance had begun to wane—began to exert pressure on him, and he stopped seeing her.

He heard everywhere that the industry he served was in the throes of an economic recession, but this did not make much of an impression on him, even when his producer friend cried havoc. One day a young actress, in whom his studio had a vested interest, turned up ailing on the set. He was summoned

and, aware that she was in the middle of an expensive shooting schedule, decided that she had a slight cold and was probably malingering. Two days later she was taken from the set in an ambulance with a virus pneumonia which she barely survived. His mistaken diagnosis cost the company a great deal of money and almost cost the girl her life.

He was fired.

If he had been able to think straight, he would have known that he deserved it. But he was resentful at what he considered a grave injustice. He charged around, talking a little wildly about setting up a private practice. He went so far as to rent office space, but attracted few patients. One of these called him in the middle of the night, but he was incapacitated. The woman suffered a miscarriage, and his reputation suffered accordingly.

His money dwindled. So did his friends. In his corner of the world, association with a failure was considered unlucky. He ran into debt and gambled frantically. One night he lost a thousand dollars in Las Vegas, and the next morning he received the intelligence, through the black headlines of the Los Angeles *Examiner*, that the starlet swallowed an overdose of sleeping pills bearing his prescription number. Though she was rescued in time, he felt degraded. The hand of death seemed to be all around him. He decided that he was unfit to practice medicine and could never do it again.

By now his whole life was unreal, so bankrupt had it become in every way, that it did not seem quixotic to him to flee the scene. He simply got in his car and drove off.

* * * * *

He drove aimlessly for several days, up through Bakersfield and over to the Needles, shunning the big highways and following small back roads, for no clear reason except that he felt like a fugitive. He stayed in motels and cheap roadside cabins, husbanding the cash he had with him.

He had lost his taste for liquor and his appetite for food, and subsisted largely on coffee. Physical exhaustion guaranteed his sleep.

"Where you headed, pardner?" an old man behind a lunch counter in northern Arizona asked him one morning.

He looked up startled. He had been about to say "I don't know," but he knew this would sound suspicious.

"East," he said.

"Better swing south," the old man said. "Winter's late, but we're liable to get snow in these mountains any day now that will clog up the roads. Better head for the desert."

"Thanks," he said, grateful for any direction. Obediently he swung south, dropping off the Great Divide at Quemado, cutting across New Mexico slantwise, toward El Paso, Texas. This was as far as he could plan. When he got there he thought he might go over the border and lose himself.

Sandra was in his mind like a thorn, but he did not think he could bring his shame to Milburn and ask her to share it. Whatever stiffness was left in him was in his neck. Besides, he didn't suppose that she would have him back.

* * * * *

There are wild and lonely stretches in the American desert where the ribbed sand, sparsely sown with low-lying black greasewood and grotesque cactus, give the traveler the weird

sense of being lost on another planet. Even in December, the sun blazed down on the arid earth, and the warm, persistent wind blew the sand grittily against the windshield and John's eyelids. When darkness caught him on the road, the stars blossomed in the infinite sky like white flowers. His loneliness and futility increased. Here there was no place to hide. One night when he was driving toward Magdalena, he was blinded by tears. He prayed then, wordlessly, for some kind of deliverance. He could not remember when he had prayed . . . not since the war.

* * * * *

The next morning, he headed for Socorro. The region was desolate, supporting nothing but hard-bitten sheep, cropping the greasewood twigs. The only houses he saw were adobe eyries, surrounded by their low-lying outbuildings, thatched sheepfolds, rude barns, and primitive corrals. The road was narrow and winding, scrawled across the bleak landscape like some wavering chirography. He did not know when he got off the main road into one of the little unmarked tributaries that wound back and forth among the small hillocks, carrying him farther and farther from the highway.

Just before dusk, he realized that he had been driving for hours without coming to the dot on the map toward which he had been forging. It must have been fifty miles since he had passed a man riding on the hindquarters of a burro. Since then he had seen no sign of life at all, and it was getting dark.

He pulled up at the side of the road and studied the map. The region he traveled was almost without towns or roads that merited inclusion in a map, and anyway, he wasn't sure where he was. He looked at the gasoline gauge and saw that the needle swung below the quarter mark. He did not think it would do any good to turn back, since he could not remember when he had seen a gasoline pump. He sat there several minutes, unable to make up his mind. It had become difficult for him to make decisions.

When he started the motor, determined to press on as long as his fuel lasted, he found that the wheels were spinning in the loose sand. There was no traction. He got out and hunted in the luggage trunk for something to put under the rear tires without finding anything. He tried his paper maps, but they were unsubstantial and disappeared into fragments, so that he no longer had even a map.

I must get help, he thought, frantic, and taking a flashlight from the glove box, he left the car and began to plod down the indefinite road, the sand slipping into his shoes and blowing against his mouth.

He lost all sense of time, and the wild and lonely landscape encompassed him. He walked for hours, and felt that he was moving in a circle. He was amazed that he kept walking and wondered why he did not lie down and wait for morning or whatever fate would bring, but he was helpless before his instincts. His mouth had gone dry, and he was exhausted. A new gust of wind battered him, and he stumbled and went down on his knees.

It was then that he saw the glimmer of light a little way off, to the right of the road. He closed his eyes, suspecting mirage or lightheadedness, but when he opened them it was still there. He struggled up and started toward it.

As he drew near, he saw that the light came from a little huddle of buildings so typical of the region—the rude

sheepfold, the corral surrounded by a stick fence, the low house, the stunted mesquite trees around the lip of a well. There was something about it that was familiar. He had a curious sensation of recognition, as if he had seen it many times, but he could not remember where.

He approached cautiously, thinking that in such lonely places men must be armed against intruders in the night. He saw the scattering of sheep sheltered under the thatched roof of the fold, moving restlessly about; two cows chewed their cuds in the barn lot, and there was a burro tied to the corral gate.

He walked up to the door of the house and knocked, simultaneously calling, "Hello!" He remembered from his childhood that people in country places so announced themselves after dark. His heart was hammering.

The man who opened the door was big and sinewy. He was a young man, with anxious blue eyes burning in a long tanned face, and he had a short brown beard.

"Come in," he said.

"I'm—er—Dr. Wallace," John introduced himself. "John Wallace, that is."

"Thank God you've come," the man said, grasping his hand. "I didn't hear the car."

John gaped at him. "I left it down the road," he said inanely.

"She's in here," his host said. "Please hurry."

John followed him through a low doorway into another room. The girl lying on the bed under the blue coverlet was already advanced in difficult labor.

"But I—" John began.

"Everything is ready," the man said. "What do you need?"

John wavered, but he had no choice.

"I must scrub up," he said, and began to peel off his coat.

* * * * *

He had no impression of the passage of time, but it must have been about two hours later that he came out, sweating and exhausted, and glowing with a wild inner triumph. Everything had been discouraging, and he had done a good, honest job, with no equipment but his knowledge and his skill. His hand had not lost its cunning!

"It's a boy," he said, and dropped down on the braided rawhide chair.

The man bent over him and grasped his hand. "Thank you," he said. "My wife—she . . ."

"She's fine," said John. "She's asleep."

The man went into the bedroom to reassure himself, and came tiptoeing back, his face luminous in the lamplight. "He's pretty little," he said, worried.

"He'll grow," John assured him, and added, feeling that the occasion called for some amenity, "I congratulate you. He's a fine, healthy child."

"You're a good doctor," the man said.

The simplicity and faith of this statement assaulted his heart. He had had fatuous praise in his time, but nothing had ever moved him as much as the man's words.

"I have to get on," he said, embarrassed. "My car is stalled down the road a piece. I wonder if you could help me start it."

"I brought it up while you were in there. It was just stuck in the sand."

"Oh, that was good of you. How far is it from here to Socorro?"

"It's only about ten miles, but I think you've been lost."

"Yes," John said. "I've been lost."

"We're a few miles off the main road here. I'll show you how to get back to it. But not until after breakfast."

"Is it morning?"

"No, but I'm hungry."

"I think I'm hungry, too," John said. He couldn't remember when he had been honestly hungry, but now he felt ravenous.

While his host fried the meat and eggs, John looked around the room. It was bare to the point of starkness, containing only the rawhide chairs and a long wooden table that supported the lamp, the cookstove with shelves over it, a safe for food and a chest for clothes—nothing but the bare necessities of life.

When he had eaten, John got up. "I must look in on the patient," he said. The man followed him into the bedroom.

The girl was awake and was propped against the pillows, cradling the baby in the curve of her arm. She had a beautiful face, a pure oval in the Spanish-American tradition, with large, liquid eyes. She smiled, and her whole being seemed alight with happiness. Her husband came and stood by her and took her free hand and held it. The look they exchanged was so full of naked love and interdependence that John was forced to turn his eyes away. The room seemed to be full of light, and he thought that the three of them, together like that, looked like one of those old primitives he had seen in some art museum or other—the eternal family.

It came to him that this was what Sandra had meant when she said what she wanted to be really married—that money could not buy what she wanted. He knew then that he wanted to see her as he had never wanted anything in his life, and that the design of his wanderings had been to bring him to her. He could not wait to be off.

"We are very happy," the man said, as if he had interpreted his thoughts. "It does not take much to make a man happy—something to do, something to love, something to hope for."

"I must get started," John said, his eyes smarting. "I have a long way to go."

* * * * *

The glimmer of dawn was lighting the east when they came out. John stared again at the little eyrie and was struck with its familiarity. His car, standing a few feet away, looked like an anachronism.

"I must pay you," his host said, "but I have no cash. We are homesteaders. Money comes hard. Would you take a lamb?"

John turned and put his hand almost affectionately on the big man's arm. "You *have* paid me," he said. "I cannot tell you how you have paid me."

"I couldn't really pay you," the man returned. "You have given me my son's life."

"You have given me my own."

"I don't understand."

"It's a very long story," John said. "Which way is the road?"

"Bear left at the next fork, then right, then sharp left. You'll see the highway."

"Good-bye," John said. "I hope to be out this way again sometime."

"I hope so. Always stop. You'll be welcome."

John paused. "You were expecting me tonight?" he said.

"Well, in view of the day it is and you not knowing anything about us. I didn't know. Maria was expecting to go to her mother's in Roswell, but it all happened so fast. Then, too, the shepherd is new here. I was afraid he might get lost or not be able to locate you. It was a miracle you got here when you did."

"I see," John said, his bewilderment increasing. "Well, good-bye again."

* * * * *

He drove off down the rutted animal track, trying to sort out his confusion. He looked back at the homesteader's establishment, searching his memory. When he looked again, the whole thing had disappeared behind one of the hillocks, as if the earth had opened and swallowed it. He shook his head and pushed on and came to the road.

I forgot to ask him his name, John thought. He felt that he wanted to keep up with these people who had so little and yet had everything.

It was daylight when he came to Socorro. He went to the hotel and booked a room, threw himself on the bed and slept. It was noon when he wakened, and he washed and shaved and walked downstairs to the desk.

"I wonder if you could tell me the name of the homesteader who lives out north of here, a couple of miles off the Magdalena Road," he said to the man behind the desk.

"I don't know of a homestead in that direction," the clerk said. "It is very desolate country."

"A tall, handsome fellow—with a brown beard."

"I don't know this man, sir. I am very sorry."

"But it's a big homestead—sheep and cattle and burros."

"I don't think anybody lives out that way, sir. It must be on the Roswell Road."

"No," John said. "I was there. I met this man. He has a beautiful wife."

"I don't know who it could have been," the clerk said. "I was born here. I do not know these people."

At this moment, John remembered what the adobe house and surroundings had reminded him of, and his skull froze.

"What day is this?" he asked the clerk.

The man stared at John's strained face. "Why, it's Christmas," he said as if to a child. "December 25th, 1950."

John sat down weakly in one of the barrel-backed chairs.

But it could not be. He had eaten and drunk and practiced medicine and shaken hands. It was sheer arrogance to presume such a thing on the basis of a low-lying house, a bearded face and a woman who looked like a Madonna! He asked the clerk, "Is there a long-distance telephone?"

"In the booth."

"Could you get me Milburn, Kansas?"

After an interval, Sandra's voice came on the wire.

"John," she said. "Where are you?" She might never have been away.

"I'm not sure," he said. "I'm not sure of anything now. Sandra, could you forgive me?"

"John, are you all right? You sound so peculiar."

"I must see you as soon as possible."

"Come home. I've been waiting."

"I will try to get a plane from Roswell. I ought to be in Wichita by night. Could you met me there?"

"I'll be at the airport. Please tell me what has happened! I've been so worried about you."

"Sandra," he said tensely. "I love you. You must believe me."

"Of course I believe you."

At Roswell, the twentieth century flowed over him. As he walked into the plane, he welcomed the familiarity of

accepted things—wings, no longer considered miraculous. He welcomed any diversion that took his mind off the questions that hammered in it. He had no real relief until he was with Sandra and had told her about it.

She took it as a matter of course. "What a wonderful thing to say!" she said. " 'Something to do, something to love, and something to hope for!' It's the secret of life."

* * * * *

Dr. and Mrs. John Wallace returned to Los Angeles a month later. Dr. Wallace set up a private practice, uphill, but dedicated. He paid his debts and answered all the questions put to him. He now has a son of his own.

He has thought many times of trying to locate the homestead he once visited on Christmas Eve. But it would be like looking for a needle in a haystack. He may be afraid he won't find it.

Of course, he would. It's right there, where it always was. The homesteader's son is four years old now and no instrument of miracles, except as every little boy is a miracle in his own way. He takes a special interest in Christmas because it is also his birthday.

When the season rolls around, his father always speculates upon the doctor who brought him.

"I often wonder about him," he says to his wife. "He was the wrong one, you know. When Juan got here with the doctor from Socorro the next morning, it was all over. Juan's old car broke down. Remember?"

"I remember."

"Nobody in Socorro ever heard of Dr. Wallace."

"I know."

"He just disappeared. Sometimes I wonder if he was real. Or if he was sent, because we needed him."

"Who knows?"

"It gives you a turn."

"I wouldn't say so," his wife says placidly. "His eyes are on the sparrow, it is said."

Being a woman, she is so accustomed to miracles that she takes them for granted.

Margaret Cousins was born in 1905 in Munday, Texas. She was a prolific author of books, such as *Ben Franklin of Old Philadelphia*, *Christmas Gift*, *We Were There at the Battle of the Alamo*, and *Thomas Alva Edison*. She was also managing editor at *McCall's Magazine*. She herself wrote many stories published by leading magazines of the day.

"Merry Christmas, Miss Blakely!"

Linda Stevens Almond

No one came near proud, stingy, and unfriendly Miss Blakely unless they absolutely had to. And even then, with fear and trembling.

But no one told little Jane Herriot, age ten, about how terrible she was, so she decided to go up to the door of the Blakely mansion with a gift—an egg.

And that gift changed everything!

* * * * *

Everybody stood in awe of Miss Blakely and said she was proud, stingy, and strange. She was a stern-visaged woman, nearing the fiftieth mile-stone, and she lived alone in a huge house with two servants. No one visited her, except, of course, a very few intimate friends, and little children actually whispered when they passed the premises.

But something happened one autumn. Jane Herriot, aged ten, with the warmest of brown eyes, the sunniest of curls, and the gentlest of hearts, moved into Miss Blakely's neighborhood. She had not heard the unpleasant tales concerning Miss Blakely, for somehow or other Jane did not hear

unpleasant things; and perhaps if she had heard, she would not have believed them. So one morning she stood for a great length of time outside the great iron fence, gazing upon the bare trees and shrubbery, and the fountain, and thinking what a delightful place it must be in summertime. Then she saw Miss Blakely come out on the pillared porch and walk slowly up and down.

I suppose she is very lonely, thought Jane. *I think I'll go in to see her someday—tomorrow, maybe, if Mother says it is all right. And I know what I'll do: I'll take her one of Julia's eggs.* Julia was Jane's pet hen, and she thought one of Julia's eggs would be quite the choicest gift she could take when she paid a call.

So the next day, after obtaining her mother's permission, Jane went to see Miss Blakely. Hannah, the kind-looking serving woman, was a little dubious about admitting Jane, but Jane assured her, with the most engaging smile, that Miss Blakely would be glad to see her and besides, she had a present which she wanted very much to give her. Then Hannah, shaking her gray head a trifle uncertainly, led the undismayed Jane into the great library filled with endless books and huge furniture.

"Sit down," she said, trying to speak coldly; but certainly she found it difficult, for Jane had such lovable ways that it took a great deal of courage for anyone to be the least bit unpleasant to her. "I'll go see if Miss Blakely will come down."

Miss Blakely came down, plainly provoked at Hannah for permitting Jane to cross the threshold, but curious to see what sort of child this was who would dare to come to her house without being invited. So she stood in the doorway, severely surveying Jane with her cold blue eyes.

"How d' ye do, Miss Blakely?" said Jane, instantly jumping up. "I've been wanting to come to see you ever since we moved into the bungalow. You know, we live now in the bungalow at the end of the street."

Miss Blakely made no reply. She continued to stand stock-still, her lips pressed in a rigid line, thinking she had never come in contact with a more forward-talking child.

"Maybe you've seen me standing outside," pursued Jane, wishing Miss Blakely would come into the room and be more sociable; "but I suppose not, or you would have called me in."

Miss Blakely narrowed her eyes. Hannah, standing slightly behind her mistress, nervously rubbed her hands, hoping against hope that Miss Blakely would not hurt the little girl's feelings.

"And I have brought you a present," Jane went on, blissfully unmindful of her frigid reception.

"Present!" Miss Blakely had at last found her voice, also her eye-glasses, for she suddenly popped them on her sharp nose and gazed at Jane a trifle more keenly. "What sort of present could you bring me, you silly child?"

Jane thought a moment. She was not altogether pleased at being called silly, but suddenly she remembered that her mother had said Miss Blakely was not used to children, so perhaps she thought they were all silly.

"I have brought you an egg," Jane announced, stepping slightly forward.

"An egg? Absurd!" Miss Blakely exclaimed. "What do you think I want with an egg?"

"But it's one of Julia's eggs, and Julia is—"

"Ridiculous!" snapped Miss Blakely, plainly exasperated. "I suppose your mother put you up to this nonsense."

"Oh, no!" Jane hastened to say, somewhat crestfallen. "Mother doesn't know I brought the egg."

"Well, no wonder you're such a bold child," retorted Miss

Blakely, "allowed to run wild this way."

"But I don't run wild," said Jane, perilously near tears. "And if you think you don't want the egg, I'll go."

"You should never have come," was Miss Blakely's sharp rejoinder. "Show her out, Hannah. The very idea of presuming to come to a place where you were not invited!" she added, more to herself than to the astonished Jane.

Hannah stepped on the front porch after Jane and very carefully shut the door and said good-bye in the kindest possible way.

"Good-bye," Jane replied, feeling very sorry that she had made the call. But she comforted herself with thinking Miss Blakely was not well and regretting that she had not asked for that lady's health. Beyond a doubt, that was the whole trouble. And the very next day, when Miss Blakely rode by in her wonderful automobile, the audacious Jane (Miss Blakely thought she was audacious) ran out, waving her hand.

"Well, what is it?" Miss Blakely asked after she had told her chauffeur to stop, and felt very much annoyed to think she would let a chit of child make her do something against her will.

"I'm sorry I went to see you yesterday," said Jane, standing on tiptoe. "But when you're well, I'd like to come again." Jane had really concluded Miss Blakely was sick. "And maybe then you will be glad to see me."

"Humph!" retorted Miss Blakely. "Go on, William."

After that, Miss Blakely kept seeing Jane, and Jane invariably nodded her sunny head and smiled and waved her hand, and the curious part was that Miss Blakely did not appear so terribly displeased. As a matter of fact, though she would not have admitted it to a living soul, it was refreshing to find someone who did not stand in awe of her. Then one day the almost impossible happened, for the automobile actually stopped at the bungalow by Miss Blakely's order and Jane was invited to go for a ride.

"I wish you would come to see us some time, Miss Blakely," begged Jane, when at last they were back, and after Jane had effusively expressed her thanks for the lovely drive.

"We shall see," answered Miss Blakely. She was wondering, as she drove away, if she had done the right thing in taking Jane out and thereby encouraging the child's extremely friendly nature. But at least she was glad she had made up for the inhospitable reception she had given Jane the day she came with the egg.

Strange things happen. Shortly after that, Miss Blakely was taken sick, and when, at length, she was convalescing she discovered she wanted to see Jane; in fact, she wanted to see her so much that Hannah was stopped from her work one afternoon and went posthaste to bring Jane. Jane explained to Hannah that her mother was out, but, as soon as she returned, she would be right up.

"Where does your mother go and leave you so much?" Miss Blakely asked a little fretfully when Jane finally put in her appearance.

"Oh, didn't you know my mother gives music lessons to lots of children?" asked Jane, drawing up a small rocker close beside Miss Blakely. "She is helping Daddy pay for our bungalow, and I'm helping, too."

"And pray tell what can *you* do to help pay for a house?" demanded Miss Blakely, her eyes dwelling curiously upon Jane.

"Well," said Jane, leaning forward and clasping her little hands, and looking straight into Miss Blakely's face, "it was this way. I saved up my money and bought Julia. She is the

most wonderful layer, Mother says, that ever was; and I sell her eggs and put the money with the money Mother makes, and you would be surprised how it counts up."

"You don't say!" briefly commented Miss Blakely.

"And Daddy says every little bit helps," Jane proceeded. "But he says goodness only knows when we will ever get it paid for, with things so high. Still, I am glad eggs are high, for when I get a whole dozen it seems like an awful lot of money."

"How was it you brought me one of those eggs when you were saving them to sell?" questioned Miss Blakely, her keen eyes fastened intently upon Jane.

"Because I wanted you to have one," promptly returned Jane. "You see, Julia is really and truly mine; and when I give away one of her eggs, I give away something that is really and truly mine and the nicest thing to give."

"I see," said Miss Blakely. "I was under the impression that children were selfish and greedy. You don't appear to be so."

Jane made no reply. She was thinking how thin and pale Miss Blakely looked, and feeling very sorry for her.

"What does your father do to make a living, Jane?" Miss Blakely suddenly inquired.

"He is the head bookkeeper at the Harvey paper-mills," said Jane; "and we are paying Mr. Harvey for our house."

"You'll be a long time paying Benjamin Harvey," observed Miss Blakely in a sharp voice. "Oh, well, that is none of my affair," she added a moment later. "Now, Jane, I am going to let you ring that silver bell on my desk, and Hannah will bring us some tea and cake."

Jane jumped up, only too delighted to obey such a pleasing order, and pretty soon in came Hannah, broadly smiling, and carrying a tray of all kinds of delightful things.

"Oh, it looks like Christmas!" tinkled Jane. "And, please, may I help you, Hannah?"

"Now, ain't she the thoughtful little thing?" asked Hannah. "Yes, indeedy, honey, you can hand Miss Blakely a napkin and her grapefruit."

Jane was so delighted that she fairly danced forward to serve Miss Blakely. Then Hannah suggested that it would be nice to draw up a small table between them, and Miss Blakely agreed that it would be more comfortable.

"What lovely times you must have at Christmas!" she said, her happy eyes traveling over the inviting repast. She did not see the scowl which suddenly grew above Miss Blakely's eyes.

"I think holidays are tiresome and stupid," Miss Blakely said abruptly.

"Yes, you do get very tired," agreed Jane. "Mother and I go so many places and do so much that Daddy says we are just no account before the day is over."

"What do you do to make you so tired?" inquired Miss Blakely, pouring the tea from a nice fat teapot.

Jane's blue eyes sparkled as she proceeded to tell of the fun she and her mother had.

"Why, we carry gifts around, just little things we have made, and of course we have to stay a little while at each place; but, oh, it's lovely! And what do you think Daddy says, Miss Blakely?"

"I am sure I don't know," answered Miss Blakely. "What does he say?"

"Well, he says if we don't stop, he is going to make us join that dreadful society somebody got up about not giving Christmas presents." Jane made a funny little grimace. "But, of course, he doesn't mean it."

"I suppose," said Miss Blakely, "you are referring to the Society for the Prevention of Useless Giving—the S.P.U.G."

"That's it!" Jane laughed right out loud, and Hannah told William afterward she did not mean a bit of harm when she said it almost sounded heavenly to hear such precious laughter ringing in that lonely house. "But the things we give aren't useless at all," Jane proceeded. "I just wish we *could* give them some useless things, and so does Daddy, for he was only funning about that society. We have some pet families—may I please pour some tea?" Jane broke off. "It's such a funny, fat pot, isn't it?"

Miss Blakely nodded in assent. Then, "What do you mean by 'pet' families?"

"Well, the ones we kind of take a special interest in," tinkled Jane. "There are the Ameses, you know, who are so awfully poor. Their father was killed on the railroad, and their mother has to be out all day working, oh, so very hard that it just hurts you to look at her. Well, of course, we have to give them what Mother calls 'practical' things. This year, Mother has knit the cunningest sweaters for the twins out of an old one of hers; and she made Horace, who is my age, two shirts out of Daddy's; and we have the nicest fix-up dress for Mrs. Ames, fixed from things you'd never believe!" Jane's lovely little face was all aglow when she lifted it to Miss Blakely's and found that lady interested in her recital. "But, still, there are many things we just *have* to buy, like stockings and gloves; and we are going to give old Mrs. Harper a bag of flour, and—"

"I should think it would bankrupt you," interrupted Miss Blakely, "considering you are trying so hard to pay for your house."

"Mother says it nearly does," Jane replied. "But, you see, we don't give much to each other."

Miss Blakely gazed upon her small guest in genuine amazement.

"You mean to tell me you do without to give to these poor families?"

Jane nodded her sunny head. "Did Hannah make these nice cakes?" she asked.

Hannah stepped forward, all smiles. "You like them, do you, honey?"

"They are just scrum—" Jane remembered she was out visiting and refrained from saying "scrumptious." Then, pretty soon, it was time to go home, and after declaring to Miss Blakely over and over again that she had never had such a perfectly lovely time, she fairly flew to the bungalow to tell her mother of her wonderful visit.

And one afternoon a week later, when Miss Blakely was strong enough to go out, she stopped at the bungalow; and Jane's pretty little mother ran out to the automobile, begging Miss Blakely to come in, and then thanking her for all her kindness to Jane.

"Tut! Tut!" said Miss Blakely, who could think of nothing else to say. Then, "Is Jane home?"

"Just back from school," replied Mrs. Herriot. "I will call her."

"I want to borrow her," Miss Blakely pursued, "for a little shopping expedition. I am not any too strong yet, and I think Jane could give me a great deal of assistance."

"Oh, dear me!" cried Mrs. Harriot, looking and acting very much like a little girl herself, "Jane will be wild with joy. Why, you are just perfectly lovely to her, Miss Blakely." And excusing herself, she hurried into the house and soon came out with Jane, who was radiant at the prospect of helping Miss Blakely

with her shopping. Then Jane kissed her mother good-bye, hopped into the big car beside Miss Blakely, and away they sped down the road.

"Now, Jane," began Miss Blakely, "I am interested in your 'pet families.' I have been ever since the day you had tea with me."

"Then maybe you will go around with us Christmas morning when we take the presents?" cried Jane, clapping her hands.

"No, I won't do that," replied Miss Blakely. "I am going to let them come to me—that is, the children of the families."

"At your house, Miss Blakely?" asked Jane, in astonishment.

"At my house," repeated Miss Blakely.

"But, Miss Blakely, are you sure—" Jane paused a moment. "You don't like children. Maybe—"

"Not as a rule," interrupted Miss Blakely, "but you set me thinking—in fact, it has annoyed me that I could not think of anything else. And I have also thought a great deal about you and your parents being perfectly willing to do without things to help those miserable people who are absolutely nothing to you."

"But it makes us very happy," said Jane.

"Very well," proceeded Miss Blakely. "And if it makes you so happy, I am going to see what it will do for me—that is, with your help. So my idea is to get a tree, Jane," she went on, "trim it beautifully, hang their gifts on it, and invite the children of these 'pet families' of yours to come to my house on Christmas morning."

Jane was fairly bubbling with suppressed excitement. "Oh, it's too wonderful!" she cried in soft ecstasy. "Why, you must be the very kindest person in the world, Miss Blakely!"

"But I am not," Miss Blakely quickly denied. "I have, however, made up my mind to find out if I have been cheating myself of something, and I hope to know this Christmas."

That afternoon the sales-people and others in the various shops looked in blank astonishment as little Jane Herriot and "stingy Miss Blakely" went about their shopping. Jane was too happy for words. It seemed too wonderful to be true to be actually buying things for the Ameses, the Hills, the Harpers and McCloskys that she had never dreamed it would be possible to give them. Occasionally, she caught Miss Blakely's hand and gave it a warm little squeeze; and Miss Blakely, who had never indulged in such an adventure, began to feel curiously warm and glad all over.

It was a very wonderful tree that Miss Blakely and Jane, with William's assistance, trimmed a few days later. There were practical gifts, to be sure, but there were certainly any number of other gifts which the S.P.U.G.'s would undoubtedly have frowned upon. Why, there were dolls, mechanical toys, horns, a wee piano for the Ames baby, an express-wagon for the twins, games, and so on and so on, until Jane declared she was dizzy in getting them straightened out. Hannah simply could not stay in the kitchen, where delicious odors came from the oven. Never before had so much fun and excitement gone on in that house.

The front door-bell pealed, and pretty soon Hannah came in to say Mr. Harvey was in the parlor and would like to see Miss Blakely for a few minutes. Miss Blakely turned sharply. Hannah's quick eyes saw the slightest semblance of color come into her pale cheeks, and then Miss Blakely did something she had never done in another's presence—she looked at herself in the mirror before she left the room.

"William," whispered Hannah, "it's been twenty-two years

this Christmas since he set foot in this house. What does it mean?"

"I'm not one to tell things that ain't my business," returned William, in an undertone, "but day before yesterday I drove her out to the Harvey paper-mills, and they talked. They did!" ended William, solemnly shaking his gray head.

"Well, I never!" exclaimed poor Hannah, sinking into a chair.

William nodded toward Jane.

"I'd say so," said Hannah. "She's bound to bring luck, bless her little heart!"

"Hannah," Jane said, turning around, "I want you to do something for me, please. Here is something I have made for Miss Blakely, and I want you to tie it on the tree early in the morning, before she comes down."

"I guess there's nothing Hannah wouldn't do for you, you little darlin'," answered Hannah, patting Jane's bright curls.

Then Miss Blakely came in, and somehow or other she seemed different from what she had been when she left the room, and her eyes held a sparkle, and there was something like a tremor in her voice when she said:

"Hannah, Mr. Harvey will eat Christmas dinner with us."

On Christmas morning there came to Miss Blakely's aristocratic front door such a crowd of chattering, laughing, happy boys and girls that the whole neighborhood was set astir. Jane and her mother and father had arrived beforehand, wishing Miss Blakely a "Happy Christmas!" and Miss Blakely declared the wash-cloths with the gay borders, which Jane had crocheted her very self, were quite the prettiest ones she had ever seen. Hannah stepped forward to thank Jane for a cunning pin-cushion; and William said never had he owned such a beautiful necktie; but, best of all, Jane had knit it. Then Hannah opened wide the library doors, and there came an uproarious "Merry Christmas!" from the crowd.

When those children actually beheld the tree ablaze with lights and a-glitter with decorations, they appeared spellbound. Not a word, not a sound came from them. They simply stood in silent awe and amazement. Nor did the grown-ups know what to do; they, too, were silent, looking at the children with blurry eyes. But Jane knew what to do.

"This tree is yours, children," she said in her direct way. "You remember I told you that Miss Blakely had a perfectly wonderful surprise for you. This is it," gesturing toward the shimmering tree, with its weight of amazing packages. "So you can hunt for your names, and when you find them, you must thank Miss Blakely, for she is about the very kindest person in the world."

"Jane!" protested Miss Blakely. Her cheeks had grown pink and her eyes were bright, and Jane's mother thought her pretty.

Then there was shouting and laughing, and Jane, right in the midst of the crowd, was helping them find their names and just as eager with delight as they when the paper was torn from the packages and the gifts revealed. Oh, what an hour it was! Never had there been so much laughter, noise, and joy in the Blakely house. Never had so much genuine happiness stirred Miss Blakely's heart.

Suddenly Hannah was having her turn. She was inviting them into the dining-room; and this time it was Jane who could not believe her eyes. There was the table with lighted candelabra, wreaths of holly encircling them, and loaded down with fruits, nuts, cakes, and candies, besides a bag at each place to be taken home to the parents. It was so wonderful that Jane

could think of nothing to say. So while they were being served, she stole back to the library to take a peep at the tree. Suddenly Miss Blakely was beside her.

"Jane," she said in a low voice, "you must have missed your name."

"Why, I didn't look for my name," answered Jane, in surprise.

"Didn't you expect anything?" asked Miss Blakely, studying the sweet, upturned face.

"Not with all this," replied Jane.

"Well, suppose you run your hand way inside the tree," suggested Miss Blakely.

Jane obeyed, bringing out a long envelope.

"Why, I don't understand," she said, with a puzzled face, as she drew out a document.

"It means, Jane," said Miss Blakely, "that your bungalow is paid for. It's my gift to you."

"Oh!" cried Jane, in breathless wonder. "But, no, it can't be, and maybe you shouldn't, and besides, I don't deserve it. I—I haven't done anything for you—oh, dear, I don't know what to say! And Mother and Daddy will not want you to do so much, dear Miss Blakely."

"It is all right, Jane," Miss Blakely said, her hand coming down affectionately on Jane's little shoulder. "I will make it all right with your mother and father, for you, my dear, have given me a priceless gift—you have shown me how to be happy in making others happy. You have given me a great deal, Jane, more than you realize, and God bless you for your happy heart!"

Linda Stevens Almond (1881–1987) was born in Seaford, Delaware. One of the leading children's authors of her day, not only did she carry on the Beatrix Potter series but also wrote the *Buddy Bear* and *Penny Hill* series as well as a number of *Peter Rabbit* books.

God Works in Mysterious Ways

Joseph Leininger Wheeler

It is morning on the Old Chisholm Trail deep in the heart of Texas. The energy-sapping heat of summer has finally receded to make room for the soft breezes of autumn. The oaks, sensing change in the air, have fashionably transformed their faded green garments into dazzling displays of gold, umber, orange and crimson.

A new energy powers in from the North.

I
ON THE BANKS OF THE TRINITY RIVER

Every young man or woman is a sower of seed on the field of life. The bright days of youth are the seedtime. Every thought of your intellect, every emotion of your heart, every word of your tongue, every principle you adopt, every act you perform, is a seed—whose good or evil fruit will prove the bliss or bane of your afterlife.

—Stephen S. Wise

"I'm so bored," she mutters petulantly.

"Bored? How could you be bored on a day like today?"

"I just am. . . . Everything bores me . . . , in fact, life bores me."

"You're a mess."

"Guess I am."

"So what's happened to the girl I used to know?"

"*What* girl?"

"The one who was always full of life; the day was never long enough for all you wanted to do, the places you wanted to see, the dreams you wanted to chase—where *is* that girl? That's my question."

"Sorry to disappoint you—but I guess this is the new me."

He stands and starts to walk away.

"Don't leave!"

"Why not? I don't like the new girl—don't like her the least bit."

"Please, don't. You've always stuck by me before—for almost as far back as I can remember. I'm . . . I'm confused. I just don't know what to do with the new me. *Please*, don't leave me."

"Oh, all right . . . ," siting back down. "But I don't like being around bored people."

"Why?"

"Oh, I don't know, perhaps because . . . , because they suck up all the oxygen in the air. They quench my love of life."

"Joie de vivre?"

"Yes, in a nutshell. But if I stay, you owe me an explanation—and you'd better make it a good one."

"If that's what it takes to keep you here, guess I have no choice."

"None whatsoever . . . I'm waiting."

Resignedly, "Oh, I guess it's because I have everything I

want, so why should I even try?"

A long silence, as he struggles for the right words. Finally, he says, "I'm speechless because it's so out of character for you to say such a thing."

"Can't help it . . . , but why should *you* care?"

"Why should I?" He gazes at a roadrunner scurrying through the shrubbery, searching for grubs.

"Seriously, Josh, why not just accept it: that this is who I am."

"It's not that simple, Abi; there has to be more to it than what you're telling me. Something . . . something *big* . . . is happening to you, changing you. Tell me what it is?"

"N-nothing."

Suddenly, a light coming on in his brain, he pounces: "Are you doing drugs?"

"What drugs?"

"You know very well what I mean! Fess up. Are you?"

"Well," grudgingly, "some. I'm so bored, is it so bad for me to get high once in a while?"

"How long has this been going on?"

"Oh . . . , quite a while, I guess. What harm can it do? It's not like I'm an addict."

"How often do you take drugs?"

"What are you, some sort of a judge?"

"Today, yes. I repeat: How often?"

Reluctantly, "If you must know: Every couple of days, whenever I need a pick-me-upper."

"When did this start?"

"Do you *have* to know?"

"Yes."

"Oh all right, about six months ago."

"Just one drug—or several?"

A long silence, followed by a word she's clearly reluctant to say—"Several."

"Just what I was afraid of."

"Come now, Josh—I'm still Abi."

"Maybe so, but you're not the girl I used to know."

"How can you be so sure? I'm not an addict—yet. . . . It's been mainly marijuana—and everybody smokes it these days."

"Not everybody."

"Well, perhaps, but most of my friends do."

"Do I know any of these friends?"

"No."

"Hm."

"So what does that 'hm' mean?"

At a loss for words, he stands up and walks over to a nearby oak and leans on it, pondering, afraid of blurting out the wrong words. A siren pierces the stillness, growing louder as a fire engine approaches; a second follows it. Then the sound diminishes, and silence is restored.

Finally, he turns to her with pain etched in his face, and says, "I'm struggling for words because I sense that you and I are at a crossroads. You have found new friends and have entered a world I cannot enter. If I say more, you're going to accuse me of preaching at you, putting you down. So I guess . . . this means—"

"Wait, Josh!"

"Yes?"

"Don't leave me! . . . I won't get mad—not too mad anyway. Just tell me why you feel so strongly about drugs."

"Oh all right." He walks back to her and rejoins her on the park bench.

Meanwhile, Abi's thoughts flounder—as they increasingly have tended to do. She's more worried than she lets on. Mainly because she senses she's on a precipice, and how he responds may end up determining all her tomorrows.

This time, the tone of his voice is downright solemn:

"Abi, you perhaps are not aware of it, but I have recently lost several of my friends to drugs—"

"Why lost? Did they die?"

"No, but as for me and friendships that have meant so much to me, for so long, they might as well have."

"Why?"

"Because . . . uh . . . the drug world is a self-contained one, and you are either in it or you are not. . . . I'm not. Nor can I ever be."

"Come on, Josh, you're overreacting. Marijuana is harmless."

"Abi, you're right in one respect: marijuana alone is not as destructive as are meth, heroin, or cocaine."

"See, I told you so."

"Bear with me, please. Are you familiar with the columnist Amy Dickinson?"

"Somewhat. What little of her I've read, I've liked."

"Well, in a recent column she addressed the issue of marijuana."

"What did she have to say about it?"

"Let's see . . . She referenced a letter from one of her readers who was married to a weed-smoker. He'd promised to quit if she'd marry him. He did not."

"And?"

"Let's see if I can remember . . . His eyes were often bloodshot. . . . He, and his clothes, reeked with the drug smell . . . his pickup too. . . . He lost his desire to work hard. . . . He'd take forever to complete a simple errand. . . . She could no longer believe anything he said. . . . And she no longer respected him—couldn't even imagine bringing a child into their home."

"Hm."

"One thing Dickinson said so impressed me that I memorized it."

"What was it?"

"Best I can remember . . . just a minute. . . . I think I've got it:

People who use weed and get baked will deny how obnoxious and boring they can be and how big an impact it has on their lives and relationships. It's no fun to try and have a life with someone who is unavailable, unreliable, impaired, and zoned out."

"Oh, come now, Josh, it can't be *that* bad!"

"It's even worse. In my talking with people who have known weed users for some time, they declare that users, over time, tend to mellow out, lose their highs and lows . . . their ambitions—and, as a result, few CEOs will knowingly employ them."

"I don't believe you! That's not true of the ones I know— You're done now, I hope."

"There's much more I *could* share with you, Abi, but I see you wouldn't believe what I'd say, so I'll just conclude with two things: Weed users tend to become dissatisfied with the drug's highs and lows—and hence turn to harder drugs such as meth, cocaine, and heroin in order to achieve new highs."

"Are you through preaching at me?"

"Almost. Speaking only for me, the deal breaker for Christians is this: anything that interferes with God's communication with us is not even to be considered, for a life without God is not a life at all."

"Enough! Enough! Go! I never want to see or hear from you again!"

Josh turns and slowly walks away, turning around but once, saying in a low voice, "But I'll continue praying for you."

"Go!" she screams. "*Leave!*"

He quickly strides up the riverbank and out of sight.

"Now, *this* is really living!"

Abi cannot remember ever being this angry in all her life. She storms into the house and up the stairs to her bedroom. Then, grabbing her car keys from off the top of her dresser, she rushes back down, ignoring her mother's concerned question, "Abi, is something wrong? . . . Abi, don't walk out on me!" Her only answer was a slamming of the door into the garage.

In seconds, her BMW accelerates down the driveway, down the street, and onto the road out of town. Once she merges onto a two-lane highway, she stomps on it, all the while muttering imprecations: *How dare he talk to me like I'm a child! Who gave him the right to lecture me! As if just a little weed is going to change my life! He doesn't know the truth—I know it because my friends have told me over and over that most drugs are harmless—* Benign *is the word Todd used just yesterday.*

Meanwhile, passing car after car, the speedometer needle sweeps past 100 on the dial, 110, 120—and still it climbs. She thrills to the acceleration: "Now, *this* is really living!" she exults. Suddenly, from out of nowhere, up ahead, a black SUV merges from a merging lane. Instantaneously, she pulls left to pass, only to discover an oncoming semitruck barreling straight for her. Ordinarily, she'd have had little problem stopping in time—but not at 130 miles per hour! Frantically, she veers right, slams on the brakes, then loses control. Time seems to stand still as she broadsides into the SUV: the smell of burning rubber, screams from within the black SUV, the loudest crash she's heard in all her life—and all is dark.

II
THE DARKNESS AND THE DAWN

As I . . . read my Bible, I found that Jesus never refused anyone who came to Him asking help. There was no record of His ever having said, "No, I won't heal you. This illness is good for your soul." Instead, He was surprisingly concerned with the welfare of men's bodies, and the Bible assures us that not only is this same Jesus alive today . . . , but that He is always the "same, yesterday, today, and forever."

—Catherine Marshall

Time passes, midnight darkness swirls. Something awful keeps reaching for her. There are moments of murky light, but each time they last but seconds before the darkness sucks her back under.

It seems like years before she dimly perceives figures around her and far-off voices—voices that ever so gradually grow louder, and light that wins out over darkness.

At last she begins to understand what the still indistinct figures are saying:

"Do you think she has a chance?"

"Not much of one."

"I've given up hope she'll ever come out of that endless coma."

"Me too."

"But, to tell the truth, maybe it would be merciful if she never does."

"True. Not much of a life—far better just to continue her sleep—and then slip away . . ."

And then, she awakens to bright lights and the concerned faces of doctors and nurses. She tries to move, but it feels as if her body is encased in concrete. *What is this?* she wonders. *A living nightmare?*

Finally, she finds her voice, but it's so weak she hardly recognizes it as her own. "What happened? Can—can—someone"—she struggles for breath before she can continue. "—someone—tell—me—what happened?"

A kind voice eventually answers her: "We're so sorry, Abigail—but you were in a terrible accident."

"What—kind—of—of—accident?"

"Car accident."

She struggles to understand . . . and to move. "Why can't I move?"

Whispers. Then . . . "Someone might as well tell her."

Someone finally does: a kind-faced nurse. "In the accident, you were hurt bad . . . *very* bad, dear."

Suddenly she shudders as memory seeps back: "Oh! Oh! Last I can remember . . . a black . . . a dark something ahead—and a terrible . . . a terrible sound! . . . Oh! Oh!"

An injected needle rescues her from thoughts too awful for her weakened body to handle. And all is dark again.

* * * * *

Weeks pass. Visitors are now allowed into her room—but only immediate family. Her mother appears unable to accept what she sees on the bed. Invariably, her face crumples and she escapes out the door. Her father remains behind but appears almost incapable of speech.

Doctors and nurses evade her ever more frantic questions by saying, "You're not strong enough yet—we'll tell you soon."

* * * * *

Spring comes at last, and outside her window, birds sing. One never-to-be-forgotten morning, she hears a familiar voice in the hallway. As he comes into the room, she attempts to smile, then says simply, "Josh."

"Yes. It's me. Finally, they decided to let me in."

"Did—you—try earlier?"

"Yes."

"How long—has it been?"

"Months."

"*Months!*"

"Yes. It has been a very long time."

"I thought so. I have no feeling below my chest . . . and I have to struggle—to speak. Will it *always* be this way? Will I always have to struggle . . . for breath?"

Searching for the right words, Josh says, "That's in God's hands, dear."

"In other words, Josh . . . , it's . . . uh . . . not likely—is that what you're trying to tell me?"

He can only nod.

"Why would God . . . uh . . . perform a miracle for *me*?" A tear trickles down her face.

Josh retrieves a handkerchief from his back pocket and tenderly wipes the tear away. Then he says, "God never holds grudges—He loves you still . . . unconditionally."

It takes a while before she continues. "It's . . . it's high time I was told the truth. That terrible crash. . . . Was anybody hurt besides me?"

"Yes."

"How many?"

"There were four: A mother and father in the front—and two small children in back."

"How badly . . . were they hurt?"

There follows a long silence. Finally, he says, "The parents were in critical care for a very long time. They're home now, and on the mend."

"And the children?"

Another long silence—a very long one.

"Are you trying to tell me . . . that neither one—made it?"

He remains mute, but nods his head.

She is overcome by a paroxysm of grief at this: "Oh, no! No! Tell me it's not true! . . . I *killed* them . . . , didn't I?"

He can only nod once again.

His heart almost breaks as he sees unutterable anguish concentrated in her face, the only part of her body she can control.

It's many minutes before she's able to speak again. Then she says, "Josh, promise me . . . , you won't desert me again. If you do—I will die."

"I promise."

"Cross your heart?"

"Cross my heart."

"You'll come . . . back tomorrow?"

"Yes."

She can only whisper, "See you . . . tomorrow."

* * * * *

"Good morning, Sunshine! Here's a bowl of flowers to brighten your day."

"Bluebonnets! How sweet! . . . Put them on that table, please—so I can look at them all the time—pretend I'm outdoors in them . . . looking up at the sky."

Then, changing moods, "Josh, be honest with me. What earthly good am I to anyone? Who cares whether I live . . . or die?"

"Your folks do—*I* do."

"I mean, other than you. . . . The folks come in each day—but they rarely stay long."

"How about your friends?"

"They don't come at all—it's like . . . to them I never was."

"How sad."

"But I mean if, Josh . . . I'm just one huge expense—to the folks. And I take up a hospital room that . . . that could be used by . . . someone with a future. . . . I have," and here her voice breaks down, "I have no future. . . . Can't figure out why those two—precious children—died. And worthless I live on . . . for what?"

"Abi—hold that thought: why the two children died . . . and you did not. No one but God could know the answer to that. I certainly don't. But let me ask you a question: In all the

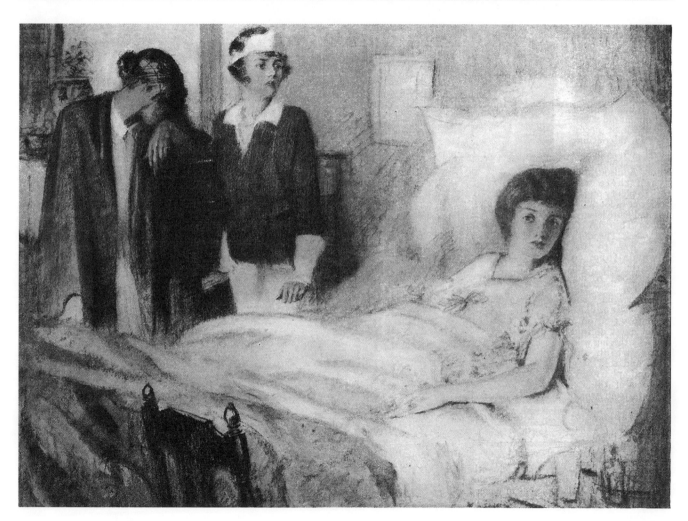

long days and longer nights of lying here inert, have you ever wondered, *What would I do differently—if I could live over the last seven months?*"

There is a very long pause before she answers, almost in a whisper:

"For starters, I . . . I wish I'd really listened—to you that day."

"Go on."

"Oh you were right . . . and I hate to admit it. . . . Had I continued as I was going . . . I shudder to think of where . . . where I'd be today. In fact, . . . bad as things are, . . . don't know if I'd change places—with the girl I was."

"You really *mean* that?"

"I most certainly do!"

"So you've forgiven me for giving you such a hard time that day? How often I've been unable to sleep at night, thinking, *If only* I'd soft-pedaled it, she wouldn't be paralyzed today."

"Yes, Josh, I've forgiven you. . . . You . . . you cared enough to be tough . . . on me. I needed it."

Noting he's incapable of speech, she continues. "You'll remember that . . . on that day, you referenced God . . . and I didn't want to hear you."

"Because?"

"Because I wanted nothing to do with Him."

"Why?"

"Because . . . deep down, I knew what I was doing . . . was wrong. Knew that drugs were, uh . . . driving a wedge between me and God. . . . I wanted *my* way—not His."

"And now?"

"Now—I realize He's my only hope. . . . But He won't . . . uh . . . give me the time of day. Why should He, after all I've done? . . . . Oh, Josh, the days are bad enough—but . . . the nights are interminable . . . seems like daylight will *never* come!"

"Lonely?"

"Unutterably—so lonely I cry and cry and cry. . . . Your visits are about the only things I have to look forward to."

"Abi, are you open to a few suggestions?"

"Of course! Anything's better than this."

"Very well. But do you mind if I have a word of prayer with you?"

"No-o."

"All right. Dear Lord, as You are fully aware, Your child Abi is feeling deserted, useless, in the way, and unutterably lonely. If it be Your will, beginning tonight, would You speak to her . . . comfort her . . . inspire her . . . show her how she might, by tomorrow morning, start making a positive difference in the lives of *every person* who comes in her door? This is my prayer. Amen."

Then, without asking her for a response, he says, "Be seeing you tomorrow evening. May God bless and guide you—" and he leaves the room.

* * * * *

Next evening, he is greeted by a radiant Abigail. She says, "Sit down, please. I have *so* much to tell you! . . . When you left so abruptly yesterday, I was angry with you. . . . After all, the great God of the universe . . . was way too busy . . . to spend time with the likes of—me. But Josh, last night, *God came into this room*—it actually lit up . . . with the glow of His presence! Instantly, I felt loved . . . cherished . . . of value to Him. He

stayed with me until just before dawn. . . . Then, His parting assignment: *Each person who walks into your room today—love that person for Me. . . . Forget self completely.*

"And I've followed His directions. . . . Lizzy, the crusty nurse who snarls each morning—when she replaces the night nurse. . . . well, this morning, I didn't even give her a chance: I smiled and said, 'Lizzie, you'll never know . . . how much of a day-brightener you are for me. Here I am . . . unable to do anything for you—yet—day after day, you do your best to bring happiness to me!'

"Would you believe it, she just stood there in shock . . . staring at me . . . as though she'd never seen me before. . . . Then she swiftly crossed the room . . . bent down and *kissed* me, saying, . . . 'Oh, you dear dear girl—I don't deserve such kind words . . . for I've been such a grouch! So can we start all over, Dearie?'

"What I discovered . . . was that God was with me every . . . step of the way. . . . Each person who came in . . . doctor, nurse, orderly—I passed on to them . . . God's love. In fact, I fairly bubbled over with joy. . . . And nobody wanted to leave! In the process . . . I discovered I couldn't outgive anyone! And all the while, I kept saying in my mind . . . *Oh, thank You! Oh, thank You, God.*"

"So tell me, Josh . . . how did you know?"

"I didn't for sure, but I've been praying almost nonstop that God would miraculously step in—meet you more than half way. . . , by the way, I'm curious: What about your doctor?"

"Oh, you'll never believe it . . . for Dr. Gronke has never been willing . . . to tell me *anything* I wanted to know . . . a real curmudgeon! Well, he melted like hot butter . . . when I thanked him for all his kindnesses . . . and for taking such good care of me. I even asked about his sick daughter. . . . Why, he didn't even want to leave the room . . . when he was paged!"

"All day long . . . I was so busy passing Christ's love on to others that I didn't have a moment to . . . in your words—mutter 'poor-me-isms!' . . . Now, don't get self-righteously smug on me," and she laughs at the boy-caught-with-his-hand-in-the-cookie-jar-look on his face. Laughs as she hasn't in well over a year.

"So, Abi, what about your folks?"

"Oh, that was the best of all! . . . When Mom edged into my room . . . like a martyr of olden times . . . , I said, joyfully, 'Mom, how kind you are . . . to spend time with me each day! . . . You'll never know how much . . . your daily visits mean to me—I'm sure I've robbed you . . . of all kinds of fun things . . . you'd far rather do . . . than visit a hospital!' Why, she rushed over . . . put her arms around me . . . and sobbed—sobbed bittersweet tears. Stayed with me hours . . . and we communed . . . like we used to do when I was a child."

"And your dad?"

She fairly sings; "When I forgot about myself . . . and thought about how I've . . . I've darkened his life . . . , I just told him how much . . . , how very much . . . , his love and care means to me."

"And—"

"Oh, he just broke down—cried like I've never heard him cry . . . in all my life! . . . And hugged me. Undemonstrative dad . . . hugged me like he *really* meant it!"

"Thank God!"

"I *do* thank Him."

* * * * *

And so begins a new life for Abi. Every day, new experiences. Every day, as word spreads down hospital halls, more nurses and doctors come in to see this miracle: a joyful caring quadriplegic. The mood of the entire hospital begins to change. Every time she laughs her infectious laugh, it seems to reverberate down all the halls.

One morning, some time later, as the day shift begins, Lizzie, whose personality has changed 180 degrees, hurries into the room of her now "favorite patient," and says, "Abi, I've been wondering about something—"

"Yes?"

"It's this: It is well known in medical circles that many quadriplegics tend to struggle for air when they speak. They have to stop often to get more air in their lungs. It has been true with you too—until lately. What's happening?"

"Oh, Lizzie, I've often shared with you my new and wonderful friendship with God, who has become my Best Friend."

"Yes, you have."

"Well, not long ago, in the middle of one of those seemingly endless nights, I made a rather strange request of God. I haven't asked Him to heal me—mainly because it is this paralysis that has revolutionized my life—and I wouldn't want to do anything to jeopardize my new life. However, on that particular night, I said, *Lord . . . , I'm not asking to be healed, but I've been wondering—people must get impatient with me . . . because it takes so long for me to get my words out. So . . . might it be Your will to grant me more breath? I'm not asking for me—but for them. Nevertheless, not my will—but Your will—be done.*

"The very next morning, it began happening: I was able to speak longer and longer without having to break for breath. Oh, Lizzie, God is so good to me!"

A *big* favor

It is August in mid-central Texas. As Josh enters her room, mopping his brow, he says, "My goodness, it's hot out there! But mercifully, it's cool in here. So how did your day go?"

"Wonderful as always. But I'm turning to you for a *big* favor—one I wouldn't ask of anyone else."

"It is yours—even unto half of my kingdom."

"Don't be silly. This is a *big* favor."

"I apologize. What is it?"

"It's this: I've been thinking more and more about the couple in the black SUV, and how they must hate me for ruining their lives. And God has been working on me. Been saying, *'My dear Abi, don't you think it's time to speak to the couple who lost their children in the crash?'* I agree with Him. How many thousands of times their reproachful broken-hearted faces have mutely spoken to me! . . . So here's my request: Would you be willing to track them down, wherever they may be, and ask if they'd be so kind as to come see me? Tell them I can't live at peace with myself until I speak with them and ask for their forgiveness. Tell them where I am, and why I can't come to them. . . . Would you do that for me?"

"I will. In fact, since they were brought here after the accident, I'm guessing the hospital will have their contact information. I'll speak to the hospital CEO himself and explain, because such private information is extremely confidential. Hopefully, he'll work with me."

In due time, it is arranged. The CEO contacts the couple, explains the situation to them, and asks if it would be all right

for Joshua to contact them personally. They (Bart and Ashley Bainbridge) agree to meet him. Several days later he visits them in their home and makes his pitch.

* * * * *

Late one September afternoon, the head nurse of the extended stay rehab annex (where Abigail has been moved to) calls out, "Knock! Knock! It's Janet. We have visitors who've come to see you. May I bring them in?"

And so the couple, hand in hand, enter the room. The only other occupants are Joshua, Abi, and her parents. Abi has prayed, day and night for a week, that God would lead in this meeting. But now is the moment of truth—can she pull it off?

As Abi studies their strained faces, the premature gray in the man's hair, all thoughts of self vanish, heartfelt sorrow and empathy taking their place. So much so that she can't speak, and the tears trickling down her cheeks do the talking for her. Suddenly, as one, the man and woman rush to Abi's bed and engulf her in their arms. Even the head nurse, just turning to leave, is deeply moved.

As the words come at last, when Abi begs for their forgiveness, the bereaved mother breaks in, saying, "Oh my dear girl, how could anyone not forgive you? Indeed, how could anyone be punished any more than you already have? Of course, Bart and I forgive you."

After a time, Ashley turns to her husband with a question in her eyes. He nods. So she reaches into her purse and lovingly retrieves a slim packet, from which she proceeds to unearth two treasured photographs. She shows them to Abi, and with a catch in her throat, says, "Bart and I have been praying a lot about this meeting with you, and we were convicted that we should have these photos of Lisa and Lowell (our twins), made from originals, in order to leave them—with you—if you should want them."

Abi, who has been staring at them transfixed, says, in a ragged voice, "Want them—*want them!* I've never wanted anything more in my life! I'll have them framed where I can look at them every day of the rest of my life! . . . I must confess something to you—" And here she glances over at Josh. "Before that terrible accident, I'd lost control of my life. My life was heading down a drugged-up road with no likely exit. Josh reasoned with me and sternly warned me of the consequences of my downward path. I was so furious at being balked that I got into my BMW and bullheadedly decided I'd show him who was master of my life. I showed him, all right. At a terrifyingly high speed, I smashed into your SUV, destroyed your dreams for Lisa and Lowell, and encased me in cement for, most likely, the rest of my life.

"God has already performed one miracle: enabling me to speak normally. The second is that God has created a new heart in me: implanting new goals in me, and transforming me from about as close to a zero as a person could ever be . . . into someone who seeks to make a difference in the lives of every person who comes into my room. And now, with these two precious photos of Lisa and Lowell always by me, every day of the rest of my life I dedicate to keeping their memories alive."

For a brief time that seems endless, no one in the room is capable of speech.

Sometime later, as the visitors get up to go, Bart, with an arm around his wife, says, "Abi, you'll never know what this day means to us. We're just now beginning to emerge from the darkest year of our lives. Also, Ashley's inability to ever have any more children—has darkened our inner skies all the more.

"But now, miracle of miracles, to find someone else who already cherishes them almost as much as we do, well, we're just overwhelmed." He glances over at Abi's parents and says, "Without diminishing in any way your relationship with your daughter, would you be willing to let us adopt her too? We just can't stand the thought of leaving this room for the last time." Then noting their murmurs of agreement, he turns to Abi and says, "Would you be willing to be our daughter too?"

"You really want me?"

All doubt is quickly removed as the new mother embraces her new daughter, and kisses her again and again.

It is a long time before Ashley and Bart leave. But they won't be gone long. They won't *ever* be gone long. Thus they leave with a spring in their steps and a song in their hearts.

* * * * *

One early October day, Josh enters Abi's flower-bedecked room and says, "My goodness! What is this? A floral shop—or a branch of Hallmark Cards?"

Abi smiles and says, "Some of it comes from you know who—and I'll never be able to thank you enough for getting them to come. . . . *So much* has happened since that wonderful day."

"Speaking of which, Abi, since I've missed so much (between college and work, I can't be here nearly as much as I wish), would you mind filling me in on events?"

"Gladly! First of all, there was that interview by columnist Catherine Blanding—"

"How did *that* happen? She's big time."

"Well—because there are no secrets in hospitals. Since the nurses and doctors spend so much of their lives here, we patients become their extended family. And vice versa, of course. Especially us 'lifers,'" smiling ruefully. . . . "Fortunately, Dad, years ago, purchased top-of-the-line disability coverage—and has deep pockets besides, otherwise—"

"Don't get off the track, Abi. Tell me more about the interview—that changes everything, doesn't it?"

"Absolutely. One morning hardly anybody knew me."

"And the next day, you were a celebrity!"

"Pretty much. Ms. Blanding was mighty good at her craft. She'd spent days interviewing people who know me—former teachers, principals, our pastor, nurses and doctors, former classmates—she was amazing! When she came into my room, it was as if she'd always known me. The old me, *and* the new me. She didn't pull punches. What she was interested in most was prying from me the story of how I'd flip-flopped from that horrid self-serving whiner into the new me. Of course that meant I had to tell her (but not reveal your name) how a long-time friend did a Dutch uncle on me."

"Guess I wasn't very subtle."

"Subtle? Like a sledgehammer!"

"However she did it, Abi, it was a masterpiece! She used your story to dig into a far deeper story: the plight of all those thousands of Americans who have been reduced to paraplegics and quadriplegics by accidents or war. It turned out to be the perfect human interest conduit into her readers' hearts. And then, TV interviewers and bloggers picked up the story."

"You're right. Far more celebrity than was good for me. But bridging to the cards and flowers, so many former friends and

classmates have resurfaced. So many who never knew me at all have weighed in. Hospital employees who . . . who . . . uh . . . who . . . love me." She struggles for equilibrium.

"And what about the Bainbridges?"

"Oh my, it's almost funny. As you know, my folks have never been very demonstrative—"

"You mean, stiff-upper-lip and all that sort of thing?"

Laughing. "Yes. Even during this last year, when they'd walk in the room it was as though they were saying, 'Abi, I'm here. It's my duty to take care of you'. . . and now here comes 'Mother' and 'Father'— as opposed to 'Mom' and 'Dad.' 'Mother,' who fairly loves me to death, bombards me with flowers, reads to me by the hour, and almost has to be shoved out by the nurses. . . . And she puddles up every time I call her 'Mother' —because, as she once put it, 'I never expected anyone to ever call me "Mother" again.' 'Father' is almost as loving as she. At any rate, 'Mom' and 'Dad,' as a result, are loosening up a bit."

Josh laughs again, then says, "Reading to you by the hour? Tell me more."

Silence. Finally, she says, "I don't quite know how to answer that. Fact is, I'm getting more and more jealous of you. You're growing mentally every day as you immerse yourself in your environmental engineering courses. . . . You're also developing career-wise in your internships. Mother quickly picked up on that one down-day and pumped me dry. So now, through her reading to me, and electronic transcriptions of stories, books, and coursework, I'm ever so gradually edging my way into a learning track."

"Why didn't you tell me? I could've helped you."

"Because, Josh, you have already done far more than your share! Why, look what I've become to you: an albatross you can't get rid of. I even made you promise never to leave me. Almost every day for the last year plus, you've taken time away from your crazy schedule to dutifully visit me and do your best to make me happy."

"Do you think for a moment that . . . that that's all you mean to me?"

"No. Your friendship means *everything* to me. But you need to also spend time with your *other* friends, and make new ones. It's in the nature of things that one of these days, . . . you'll want to find the one you've been looking for. Marry. Have a family. . . . I recognized some time ago that such a future, short of a miracle, can never be for me."

He is speechless, for they've never gotten this personal with each other before. And here, in just a few minutes, Abi has almost brutally articulated her new realities. For he'd never told her he loved her. He'd never proposed. He'd never done anything—anything that is—but be the one steadfast friend in her life. The one she could *always* depend on. As faithful as day following night, and night following day. He doesn't know how to answer her.

Recognizing the blow to his inner solar plexus, she takes pity on him, and says, "Don't even try to answer that. It's taken me a long time to say it, but I've been thinking about it for many weeks now. It shouldn't change anything, for our friendship is too strong, too enduring, to be at risk just because it's not likely to rise to a different level, different dimension. . . . Good night, dear."

For her, it is another very long night. *What have I done?* But she knows full well what she's done: beat him to it. Sooner or later, it is the nature of things that it will surface in his own

mind. And she knows that pity is no valid substitute for love. He'd begin to feel boxed in, with no graceful way out. Far better to articulate these realities herself.

The turning point

November makes way for December, and her hospital room is decorated for Christmas. The previous December, she was in no condition to celebrate Christmas, but this year, she is. Dr. Gronke's little girl, Melanie, has heard her dad talk so much about this special patient that she asked if she could visit her. It is arranged, and the result is that a real bond develops between the two. Melanie, a confirmed Christmasaholic, asks if she might help decorate Abi's room. Of course, the answer is yes.

It isn't long before it's the prettiest room in the hospital Not content with that, Melanie gets permission to bring in her third-grade friends and sing Christmas carols to the entire hospital—but, of course, they sing longest in Abi's corridor.

Then a new year dawns. But it is different, for now, thanks to Josh's efforts, Abi is enrolled in a collegiate adult degree program, double-majoring in English and elementary education. Thanks to her four-pack of parents, tending nurses, and, of course, Josh, she has plenty of help in her learning process.

One night, shortly after midnight, Abi dreams she can move her fingers. The dream sequence is so wonderful she doesn't want to ever wake up. When she does, around 5:00 A.M., she discovers it's only a dream. Nothing has changed. But as she begins her morning devotions, she's impressed to say:

Dear Lord, it's Your child Abi once again, with a request. Josh has been sharing with me many healing-related passages in the New Testament. We both couldn't help but notice that, while You were on earth, and individuals with incurable medical problems—even several with paralysis—well, they came to You, or were brought to You, and You were kind to them all. Healed them all. Because of this, I feel emboldened this morning to make a similar request: Lord, I believe You can heal me if You want to, just as You did with the leper in Luke 5 and Matthew 8. When the leper said, "Lord, if You want to, You can make me well again," and You reached down, touched him, and said, "I want to. Be healed!" he was. So Lord, I ask this in faith—I know for a certainty that You have the power to heal me . . . if You want to. Thank You, Lord.

And her fingers move again—only this *is* no dream!

* * * * *

As days and weeks pass, more and more feeling and functionality slowly return to her fingers and hands. Then came that wonderful day when she is able to sit up by herself, pick up a pen, and write a word! And now her prayers are paeans of joy and thankfulness. Dr. Gronke can hardly contain his amazement!

One April morning, as spring takes out her palette and begins painting the Old Chisholm Trail bluebonnet blue, Abi hears a Voice she's come to love and cherish. In a tender but firm voice, He says, "Child . . . stand up!" Abi (knowing that Christ, while on earth, almost invariably asked those who asked for healing, to show their faith by overt action) dares

not refuse the divine command. Almost like it was something dreamed, her feet come alive, she moves them out from under the covers, she stands and—she can't *help it*—she *screams!* And nurses rush in to see what has happened—only to discover her standing up by her bed, tears of joy running down her cheeks. Dr. Gronke, coming by on his morning rounds, hears her scream and rushes to her room—just in time to see her standing without any support.

He is totally silenced. There is a look of awe on his face as he looks up and reverently says, "Lord, *I believe!* Please forgive my unbelief!" And then nurses and doctors begin pouring in from all over the hospital. Mom, Dad, Mother, Father, and Josh are summoned and told to hurry to the hospital—no explanations given. They rush to their cars, fearing the worst; and fear even more when they see the crowds of people. People smilingly part to let them through—only to see the miracle themselves!

From then on, almost every day sees gathering strength in Abi's back, hands, and feet. The media trumpets the story, and the whole city celebrates!

And so a new Abigail is born, shorn of all her earlier self-centeredness and drug abuse. And what a celebration it is the day she is able to walk out of the hospital on her own two feet!

III
A DIVINE SHIFT ON A RIVERBANK

Woman was made from the rib of man.
She was not created from his head to top him.
Nor from his feet to be stepped on.
She was made from his side to be equal to him.
From beneath his arm to be protected by him.
Near his heart to be loved by him.

—*Quoted by Ann Landers (7-30-86)*

Life is now so full with Abi that there is far less time for reflection, especially after she swaps independent study for on-campus classes. She is equally popular with both sexes; however, young men swarm around her. With her love for God shining through in everything she does, with her inner beauty seeping into her external beauty, with her joie de vivre the capstone, she is, in a word, irresistible. But she makes it clear that the drug-abuse period of her life is far behind her. The dates she accepts are, without exception, with those who share her Christian values.

Part of the pattern of her new life is that every second week she has a luncheon date with Mother and Father, sometimes in their beautiful home overlooking Lake Hubbard, and sometimes in area restaurants. She finds them to be kindred spirits, far easier to turn to for counsel than has ever been true of her biological parents.

One evening about sunset, seated in comfortable chairs by picture windows overlooking Lake Hubbard, Mother, with a pensive look on her face, asks her a rather jolting question: "Abi, we're both curious. In times past, you and Josh were together almost every day, then less and less—now we rarely see you together anymore. Are you no longer friends?"

Abi is startled, hardly knowing how to respond. "I guess it's true we don't see each other much these days. We haven't had any disagreements. . . . I've just been so busy I didn't even notice he didn't come by much anymore, or that we were gradually drifting apart."

Bart sticks his oar in with, "We're not trying to pressure you or back you into a corner on this, but Josh has been there for you for so long it really surprised us to see you dating others but not him.... After all, he was the one who brought you into our lives."

"And," adds Ashley, "you should have seen him when he first rang our doorbell! My, he was nervous! Reason being, he was so afraid he'd fail in getting us to come see you in the hospital. For good reason, because we actually hated you for destroying all our dreams for our children. It took him well over an hour to break through our icy hatred."

"Besides," says Ashley in little more than a whisper, "by the time Josh left us, not only was our hatred gone but we loved you even before we walked into your room—so it's no wonder he's become ever dearer to us in the year that followed."

Then Bart says, "Ashley, why don't you tell Abi what it was that you said to me after Josh left our house."

Laughing, Ashley replies, "Oh, I just idly remarked, 'That young man may not realize it, but, unless I miss my guess, he's deeply in love with that girl.' "

Abi doesn't know what to say, mainly because Josh *was* no longer present in her life. Finally, she answers, "I can't give you any good reason, Mother . . . it's just that he doesn't come around much anymore . . . and I guess I've been too busy to notice."

"When," queries Bart, "did this cooling off of your friendship take place?"

"Let's see . . . Oh, I know! It was after he shopped around, studying area adult degree programs, and then helped me enroll in the program he felt would be best for me."

"So did he just quit coming around then?"

"No. . . . He still came around . . . but, more and more, I was too busy. I can see that now: he must have grown tired of my unavailability—how cruel of me!"

"I'm wondering, dear, if perhaps he began to feel that since he was no longer essential to you on a daily basis—that you no longer needed or valued his friendship," adds Ashley.

And then the conversation moves on to other things.

But Abi can't so easily get the subject out of her head. True, she'd once told Josh that there would be neither romance nor marriage in her future—but that was before the great miracle: *Which brings me to the big question: Among those I'm dating today, is there one I'd consider seriously as a fiancé, and possibly more? There's no question: Not one!*

What about Josh? I don't really know, because we've never— even brought up the subject of romance between us. It has been friendship—and that alone, so how could I know if there is any real chemistry possible with him? But I do know one thing: it's long past time to mend that friendship!

She invites him to attend a church social with her. He seems surprised, hesitates, then says, "Sure."

Afterward, as he walks her home, there is tenseness in the air. Never before has she felt dissonance between them or obstructions keeping them from being at ease with each other. Finally, fearing she might lose her last chance to salvage what once she'd taken for granted, she stops, and with a tremble in her voice, says, "Josh, I have an apology to make."

Surprised, he says, "For what?"

"For permitting my busy life to jeopardize the most important friendship in my life."

A smile works its way, by degrees, into his face. "Then, are you suggesting a remedy?"

"Most definitely: I want our friendship back—only this time I won't be such an ungrateful wretch!"

"Sounds good to me. When? Where? Your choice."

"No, this time it's *your* choice. I'm taking no chances."

* * * * *

And so their friendship resumes, but it's now different, because both of them are aware that the subject of actually dating each other has never come up. And neither one is willing to jeopardize the restored friendship by bringing it up.

Weeks pass, then months. Yet the subject of something more than friendship never surfaces.

Another day on the Trinity

It is autumn once again at Trinity River Park, and side by side they stroll down along the riverbank, swans sailing like windjammers down the river, and proud oaks preening over their crimson reflections.

Abi breaks into his thoughts by saying, almost in rapture, "Oh, Josh! How thankful I am for all God has done for me—given me back a life! And the chance to make a difference in the world. I can hardly keep my feet on the ground, I'm so happy."

But Josh's thoughts do not mesh with hers: *Though it's wonderful to have been part of her miracle, I can't help but wonder, now when everything is going right in her world, where do I come in? For so long I had to be the strong one, not missing a day of her life. . . . But now she doesn't need me anymore. . . . When I'm with her, for the first time ever, easy speech fails me.*

Abi, having spent so much time in Josh's vicinity, can read him like the proverbial book. She breaks into his reverie by saying, "I can never thank you enough, Josh, for all you've done to salvage me—not if I lived a thousand years! Quite simply, it's a debt I can never repay."

But I don't want to be repaid! he inwardly responds. *I'm all at sea—for so long have I blocked out anything other than friendship in our relationship that I seem unable to bridge to something more than that. . . . Now that she's attending classes at the university, she's being mobbed by the guys. And I can't do a thing about it. Oh, Lord, what can I do? What can I say?*

Abi, on the other hand, wonders, *Oh my, how can I ever get back on Josh's wavelength? I can't ever remember feeling at a loss for words with him before. Best friends—but no more—that's what we've always been. Lord, is friendship all that Josh and I will ever share—or might there someday be something more?*

Suddenly, out of the blue, a fleeing jackrabbit dives between her legs; then a massive German shepherd just yards behind, slams into her, knocking her off her feet. It is so sudden, she completely loses her balance and falls at an awkward angle—and can't get up. Her left cheek is bruised, and she's in pain.

"Oh! Oh! Josh. My ankle hurts! It must be sprained, I think. No, I can't possibly get up."

"Abi, let me help you. You can't stay there in that position. I'll need to move you over to that big bench under the cottonwood. Just put your arm around my neck and I'll pick you up. . . . There, that's fine. I'll move you gently as I can."

She's amazed at how strong he is, carrying her as easily as if she were a small child. Never can she remember being held

this close to him. And yes—he smells good too.

He soon reaches the bench, but rather than placing her on it, he sits down and cradles her on his lap. Breathing raggedly, he says, "This is just too good an opportunity to miss. In fact, after waiting twenty-one years for this, now that I've made a prisoner of you, I see no good reason to ever let you go."

Smiling through her pain, she murmurs so softly he has to bend down closer in order to understand her words, "So who said I *wanted* you to ever let me go . . ."

His lips close off whatever else she might have said. That kiss goes on for a very long time. Finally, he releases her and says, "Guess this calls for a few formalities: I've been in love with you forever, but until lately, I couldn't tell you so. Then it seemed like I'd never have the chance to find out if you loved me."

She pulls his head down and says, "Dearest Josh, if that kiss didn't answer your question, I guess I ought to be a bit clearer—" and kisses him on her own terms.

* * * * *

And the world has changed for both of them.

One Christmas afternoon

After the most deeply moving Christmas Eve Abi can ever remember, complete with memories shared, Christmas stories told, Christmas music played and sung, and then testimonies and prayers of gratitude, all wearily retire for the night.

Neither the bride nor groom are in evidence on Christmas morning. It's midafternoon before carloads of family find their way to the largest church in the region. A vast crowd slowly assembles, media too, for Abi is undoubtedly the most beloved young woman in the city.

As evening shadows fall, an organist begins a Christmas Evensong; later in comes a children's choir, each child walking down the aisle with a candle, the only lights in the church being the candle flames—the audience sitting in absolute reverent silence.

Then comes the seating of the bride's two mothers by the groom, one on each side as he walks them down to the front—then he seats them together on the same side of the church. He then goes back for his own mother.

Anticipation grows as word gets around that this is going to be a very different wedding.

Then a hush as the first of a long line of groomsmen, some hospital doctors, some hospital male nurses or aides—all wearing their hospital attire, and each carrying a candle—slowly and reverently walk down to the front, mount the platform, and spread out across half the width of the church, to the right of the groom, the best man (Dr. Gronke) and the minister.

Another hush before an equally long line of nurses, and aides, each wearing their nurse caps and attires, each carrying a lighted candle, move slowly down the aisle and fill the other half of the platform next to Lizzie, the maid of honor.

After all have positioned themselves at the front, all the groomsmen light the candelabras at the front on one side, and all the bridesmaids the candelabras on the other side; then all return to their positions. It seems to the audience that the city's hospital must be all but deserted on this night.

Rustling and much craning of necks precedes the pièce de résistance. First: the flower girl, Melanie, of course, scattering flower petals from side to side, and by her side, her little brother,

Bertie, solemnly carrying the Bible; and just behind them, Melanie's third-grade choir, also carrying candles and singing "Silent Night," just as they had sung it in the hospital corridor at Christmas a year before—for this is Christmas Night.

Finally, a vision in white appears at the door, escorted by Dad on one side and Father on the other. Abigail is almost overcome by it all, and she trembles as she takes that first step. Holding her long train are two little neighbor girls. Noting her trembling, both fathers protectively tighten their hold on her arms. Everyone stands. Then comes the long walk down the very long aisle, to the sounds of Wagner's "Bridal Chorus" played by a master of the pipe organ. Way down at the end of the aisle is the face of an adoring groom, almost overwhelmed by the loveliness of the bride, and by this thought: *What a miracle to see Abi walk toward me. . . . Thank You, Lord.* Finally, Joshua claims her from the two fathers, and bride and groom ascend the steps together.

Dr. Gronke turns out to be master of ceremonies. In his wedding homily, he tells those assembled the incredible story of the last three years of the bride and groom. He references the fact that long-term friendship paved the way for love. Then he clears his throat, wipes his glasses, and tells the story of the miraculous healing. He concludes with these riveting words: "One moment, I was at best a nonattending Christian. *Moments later, I was a devout believer in an almighty caring God! Truly, God moves in mysterious ways His wonders to perform!*"

The minister (Abi and Josh's church pastor) then lovingly ties the knot so tight not even an earthquake could pull it apart.

Then that always unforgettable moment when the bride and groom turn around and, hand in hand, listen to the minister say—in this case: "Ladies and gentlemen, it is my great privilege to present to you, as husband and wife, Joshua and Abigail Hudson."

Immediately, the church bells begin to ring, and thanks to a great deal of arm-twisting by Bart and Ashley, one at a time, every church bell across the great city joins in the joyful clamor.

And Joshua and Abigail walk out of the first Christmas of the rest of their lives.

* * * * *

How this story came to be

First of all, like Jacob of old, I had to struggle every step of the way. All year long, I prayed that God would grant me the characters and the plot so that I could finish early. Not a chance! Finally, around a month before the book deadline, I told the Lord that the time had finally come. As usual, I reminded Him that I would not move an inch until He gave me the subject and characters. After much prayer, I became convicted that the protagonist should be a person who was self-centered and agnostic in attitude. Our son Greg, who rarely ever suggests plots to me, did this time: "Dad, have you ever thought of writing a story about a rather obnoxious person who is paralyzed in an accident or battle of some sort—and then is forced to think seriously about life?" Since I'd been thinking about such a possible topic for some time, I took the matter to God.

Then came the setting: Central Texas, where we'd lived for fourteen years. The protagonists came harder. It took a number of days until they came to me: Abigail (Abi) and Joshua

(Josh). For several weeks (night and day, awake and dreaming), my mind refused to shut off. I had, of course, no guarantee that God would keep the story going. Again and again, I came to dead ends: (1) What kind of narrative sequence would it take to reach paralysis? (2) What would it take to transform Abi's character? (3) How might Josh develop as an independent likable character when he was ostensibly brought in merely as a foil for Abi? (4) How might Abi be miraculously healed without violating the laws of probability and biblical compatibility? (5) God impressed me to reread Catherine Marshall's biography, *A Man Called Peter*, for her personal memories of her three-year bout with depression and tuberculosis and how God healed her, and the deep personal relationship with God that developed in the process. (6) God also brought out of nowhere the solution as to how the friendship between Abi and Josh could be transformed into love without significantly lengthening the story: a jackrabbit and a German shepherd—completely out of the blue: who'd a thunk it?

The fact that I had worked for a hospital myself (1984–1985) helped give the medical section verisimilitude.

Then there were my pro bono readers: Ellen Francisco, Sheree Parris Nudd, Linda Steinke, and Greg Wheeler. Because of their brutally frank critiques, I ended up rewriting much of the manuscript. Especially did the persona of Josh get a major makeover. Thirty years ago, I was convicted by God to dedicate two years of nights and weekends to collating from three decades of reading the most powerful quotations I'd ever come across. From that oft-used source, I found the perfect lead-in quotes for two of the three sections.

Again, I was so afraid of being presumptuous about the plot that I didn't even let my wife Connie see it until I wrote the last word of the last sentence. And since God was the narrator, not me, I didn't know myself how it would end until that last line flowed out of the last of the half-dozen Pilot pens it took to complete the manuscript (including rewrites).

Thank You, Lord, for this story!